SUMMONING
the
DEAD

SUMMONING
the
DEAD

TONY BLACK

BLACK & WHITE PUBLISHING

First published 2016
by Black & White Publishing Ltd
29 Ocean Drive, Edinburgh EH6 6JL

1 3 5 7 9 10 8 6 4 2   16 17 18 19

ISBN: 978 1 78530 044 8

This novel is a work of fiction. The names, characters and
incidents portrayed in it are of the author's imagination. Any
resemblance to actual persons, living or dead, events or localities
is entirely coincidental.

A CIP catalogue record for this book is available from the
British Library.

Typeset by Iolaire, Newtonmore
Printed and bound by CPI Group (UK) Ltd, Croydon, CR0 4YY

For Mary Black

Prologue

November 1984

The farm road was pitted with potholes and loose scree washed down from the hills. Beyond the encroaching bramble bushes were the low-hanging branches of trees. At their thickest, the branches and the creeping bushes made a connection to their counterparts on the other side of the road, creating an arbour. Although the scrub was dense, it was not thick enough to provide shelter from the heavy rain that poured from the night sky.

The uneven road, no more than a track really, with its dents and declivities made for heavy going in the Transit van. Inside the vehicle, beyond the rain-battered windscreen and the furiously pumping wiper blades, the men cursed the job that had brought them out in such conditions.

'I swear the weather's better back home, and that's saying something,' said the driver, his mate next to him nodding in agreement.

'Just go easy. I don't want to return this van with a broken axel – it's costing us an arm and a leg as it is.'

'I'm doing my best. It's pretty bloody choppy out.'

The needle on the rev counter danced as the Transit struggled, its wheels slipping in the mud.

'I said watch it!'

'I am. I am.'

The voices were rising, along with the tempers. The larger of the two men removed his hat and started to strangle it in his hands. As the van progressed, rounded the bend at the top of a small brae and drew to a halt outside a farmhouse the tension in the cab was palpable.

'This it?'

'Must be. I don't see anywhere else.'

'We should try the door.'

'There's no one in, I told you.'

'We should try it anyway. You know what these places are like. The people are hillbillies – point a shotgun at you soon as look at you.'

The driver reached for the door handle. 'Do what you like. I'm going to find what we came for.'

The rain was almost horizontal, backed by a strong westerly that threatened to take a man off his feet. The gable end of the farmhouse offered little shelter, the big man plastering himself to the sandstone and edging along slowly, so as not to be blown over by a freak gale.

The other man turned up the collar on his black reefer coat and faced the elements. He headed beyond the farm-house, towards the outbuildings. When he reached the first of the small stone buildings he raised a hand to shield his eyes and shouted to his partner.

'It's here!'

He couldn't hear the reply, drowned out by the wind and rain as it was.

The man moved off again, content that the other man knew where to find him, and negotiated the steps to the rear of the first outbuilding. As he peered over he leaned the toe of his boot on the rim of a large oil drum; it didn't move. He crouched lower, still holding the wooden rail that skirted the steps, and pressed his weight against the drum.

'What in Christ?' he said, the words trailing before being taken by the wind.

His friend reappeared. 'There's nobody there.'

'I told you.'

'I wanted to check.'

'Are you happy now?'

'I am, yeah.'

The man in the reefer coat stood up again. 'I don't know how anyone can be happy out in this.'

'I didn't say I was ecstatic. I'd sooner be on my way home to the Dumbarton game at Pittodrie.'

'Stuffing the 'Gers 2–1 at Ibrox not good enough for you?'

They smiled, the talk of their team winning thawing the tension. Aberdeen were on a winning streak; the gaffer had done wonders with the team. No one could really believe they had only recently been European champions. Would that ever sink in?

The pair had trailed their team around the country on an old trawler, chasing cod and odd jobs along the way. But the experience, initially so exciting to their ears, had worn thin as the odd jobs got even odder.

'I can't move it,' said the man on the steps. 'I can't budge it an inch.'

The bigger man walked around the barrel, stalking it

like a strong man facing a lifting challenge. He tested the steel with his toe, as his friend had earlier. It sounded solid.

'What's in it?'

'I was told not to ask.'

'Was that wise?'

'I didn't care. Look, they were paying cash, you had your share and now we have to dump it.'

The big man gripped the drum, put a shoulder lock on the rim and heaved. 'Are you sure this is the right one?'

'Of course it is. There's the ICI badge and the cross painted in green, like he said.'

They wrestled with the barrel together, managed to tip it on its side. The ground shuddered a little as the heavy barrel splashed down in the mud.

'It's going nowhere. The bloody Transit won't move with that in it, if we could get it in.'

'I don't suppose we'll manage to get it on the boat either, not without a pulley and winch.'

'We'd snap the cable – and sink the boat.'

'That's that then. Bollocks to it.'

'We can't leave it. We've been paid up.'

'Have you got a better idea?'

He looked around. The rain was coming straight down on their heads now, bouncing in stair rods off the wet ground. 'We'll bury it here.'

'What?'

'Not right here, over there.'

'In the fields? The first time someone runs a plough over it the bloody thing will stick out.'

'Between the fields then. We roll it over and bury it as

deep as we can. No one will see it, no one will know and your man will be none the wiser.'

'I don't know about this. Maybe I should call him. I saw a phone box back on the main road.'

'You know what he'll say – you took the money, now do the job he paid us for.'

'We could give the money back. I never liked the sound of this anyway.'

'You don't give money back to people like that. Forget it. We bury it and walk away. We won't be back this way again, so it's not our worry.'

The man brushed the pooling water from the shoulders of his reefer coat. The action caused a shiver to enter him. 'What do you think's in it?'

'I don't know, and I don't want to know.'

The shivering passed. He pointed back the way they had come. 'I saw some shovels over by the barn. We'd better get started, it'll take forever in this rain.'

1

Present day

Detective Inspector Bob Valentine struggled with the blue shoe covering, the elastic stretched to its snapping point. He knew he should sit down, take his time, but that would mean admitting to himself that the spreading paunch above his belt really did require his attention.

He leaned against the wall. The morgue tiles were cold on his back and another reminder that he was somewhere that he really did not want to be. He told himself that the corpse on the mortuary slab through the wall held no fear for him. At least, that's how it had always been. Until now.

'Bloody things.' He finally managed to get his last brogue covered and sighed towards DS Sylvia McCormack, who was waiting by the door, smirking slightly.

'Something funny, detective?' he said.

'No, sir. Well, maybe a little.' McCormack took a few steps towards him. 'Have you thought about losing a couple of pounds? You'd feel the benefits of it.'

'I'm not carrying any weight, Sylvia.'

'Yes, sir.'

He rubbed his stomach. 'It's dyspepsia.'

The smirk was back. 'Boss, you'll be telling me it's the job next.'

'It is the bloody job! Well, this case.'

'Certainly seems to be making you irritable.'

The DI eased himself off the wall, rubbing his stomach. 'Bad guts is no laughing matter. I wouldn't wish it on anyone, well, maybe just Dino. I mean, what does she expect us to find here?'

'Cause of death.'

'Apart from the blindingly obvious. There's no foul play involved, we're all agreed on that. It's only the media interest that has her rattled.'

Sylvia motioned towards the door. 'They did feature it on *Crimewatch*, sir.'

Valentine shuffled his feet, made a show of distaste for the blue coverings. 'And why was that? Not because it was a pressing crime that required the vigilance of the public to solve.'

'No, sir.'

They walked towards the morgue door; Valentine held it open for McCormack to enter first. 'No, it was more to do with the CCTV from the hotel going viral. Cheap opportunism on the part of the programme makers. They're not interested in justice or protecting the public – it's ratings they're after.'

As they headed towards the centre of the room two men, dressed in white scrubs, waited beside a large, steel-legged table. Immediately Valentine identified the taller of the two as the pathologist.

'Hello, Wrighty,' he said.

'Bob . . . Sylvia,' he nodded. 'Here to get the low-down on our superstar?'

'Give it a rest.'

'I'm serious. Half a million hits on YouTube this lad got; that's up there with Oscar winners in my book.'

Valentine turned to McCormack. 'You see what I mean? We live in tawdry times. Everyone's chasing celebrity! Even Wrighty's excited to meet the Thin Man.'

The pathologist stepped aside and made a show of whispering into Valentine's ear. 'Do you think it would be OK to take a selfie with him, Bob? Nothing tasteless, just for Twitter and that.'

The DI's expression soured; he looked ready to break into a tirade.

'Bob, I'm pulling your plonker,' said Wrighty. 'Bit of gallows humour, so to speak.'

'I'm laughing inside, I can assure you of that.'

The team assembled around the table and watched the pathologist go to work. His first incision on the corpse marked the beginnings of an inverted Y, from the sternum through to the top of the stomach.

Valentine felt his own insides tightening as he watched; his stomach pains had intensified to the point where he had to place a steadying hand on the slab's rim.

'Everything OK, Bob?' said Wrighty.

'Just this indigestion.'

'You had that when I spoke to you on Monday as well. You aught to get that checked out.'

'Is that a medical opinion? If it is, I'd like to ask when you last had a live patient?'

DS McCormack had been scrutinising the organs the

pathologist removed from the body when she interrupted the banter. 'Can I ask why they're so shrivelled?'

Wrighty looked up. He had his hands under the swollen, reddish ball of the stomach. 'Probably the chemotherapy.'

'He'd been treated for cancer?' said the DS.

'Yes. Though not recently. These organs are riddled with it. By the look of it, I'd say the tumour was in the stomach and the cancer spread.' He called for an aluminium dish to place the latest removal in; the assistant took the dish away and laid it with the other organs.

'Anything you can tell us is a help,' said Valentine. 'We've no dental, and he's not on any DNA databases.'

'I saw that on the telly the other night. They said he'd removed all the labels from his clothes too.'

'Cut them out.'

'What was all that about?'

'It's common enough for suicides, when they don't want to be found. There was a French lad who went up the hills that had done the same a few years back. Took Northern an age to track him down.'

Wrighty paused and looked at the officers. 'It's a sad business. I take it that's what all the CCTV footage was about as well?'

'Every time he left the hotel the cameras in the foyer caught him with a carrier bag. The street cameras caught him putting it in the bin a few times. He was disposing of all his effects because he clearly didn't want to be identified after death. He probably never dreamed the tide would carry him back in either, and now here we are poking about in his last days and hours in the hope of undoing all his hard work.'

9

The pathologist summoned his assistant and started to remove his gloves. 'Well, I'm afraid I can be of little help to you. There's nothing to suggest foul play here. I'd say entirely natural causes, likely a massive cardiac arrest as a result of the pressure the swim had put on his heart. He was a very sick man; his organs are riddled with cancer. He wouldn't have lasted much longer even if he hadn't gone for a dip on Ayr beach.'

Valentine allowed himself a half smile. 'Well, that's that then. Nothing to see here, Sylvia, write it up as natural causes.'

'And what about his family, boss?' she said.

'What family? We don't know he has any. We don't even know his name.'

'It just seems so, I don't know, sad and mysterious.'

'And that's what it will remain, I'm afraid. We can't solve them all; we wouldn't have a station full of cold cases if we could.'

'It seems so final.'

'It is. Unless we get a call out of the blue, we don't have the resources to scour the globe for potential relatives. Don't be downhearted, Sylvia, it's just the way it goes.'

'We can't win them all.'

'Sometimes it's a miracle that we win any of them at all, you know that.'

'Yes, boss.'

The officers thanked the pathologist, shook hands and headed back to the car. Outside the morgue door Valentine removed his blue shoe-coverings without effort. 'Would you believe it? I think my dyspepsia has gone. No, it definitely has. Completely vanished.'

'I'm glad to hear it. Maybe your bad mood will have went with it. You've been like a bear with a sore head – I mean stomach – all week.'

The DI pointed the key at the car and opened the door as the blinkers flashed. Inside he turned to McCormack and said, 'Don't you think that's odd?'

'What?'

'That I've lugged around bad guts, just as we're investigating the Thin Man.'

'Who we discover today had stomach cancer. It's a coincidence of sorts. You'll be telling me you're getting the dreams again.'

Valentine turned to face McCormack. 'Who said they'd stopped?'

'But I asked you just the other day and you said . . .'

'No, Sylvia, you asked if I had had any dreams about the case.'

'And you said you hadn't. Are you telling me that's not the whole story now?'

The DI tapped the car keys on the rim of the steering wheel and looked away from McCormack. 'I did see the Thin Man in one of those intense dreams.'

'And what?'

'Nothing. Well, nothing about the case.'

'He clearly told you something.'

Valentine shifted to face the DS once again. 'He was there, on Ayr beach, and he said he had a message for me.'

'Go on.'

'He said I had no need to worry because, when it was my time, my mother would be there to take my hand.'

11

'That could have been just a dream, you know.'

'I told you, they're not like dreams at all.'

'Maybe we should have another meeting with Hugh Crosbie.'

'Who?'

'The psychic, spiritualist bloke that Colin Baxter – the precognitive – put us in contact with before. He might have some insight.'

'I'm not sure about that.' Valentine put the key in the ignition and reached for his seat belt.

'Why not?'

'I don't know whether he was a help or a hindrance the last time. There's some things you're better off not knowing about.'

'That sounds like denial to me. Aren't you getting dangerously close to burying your head in the sand?'

He paused. 'Maybe you're right. I'll think about it.'

'OK, but don't come crying to me when you're toppled over with stomach pain again, or worse, maybe headaches from a victim of a shotgun blast!' McCormack kicked her bag into the footwell.

As Valentine started the engine the radio came to life. The voice of Jim Prentice on the control desk sounded stressed, directing officers to a rural location.

'I know that place,' said Valentine.

'Sounds like a farm.'

'That's exactly what it is. Ardinsh Farm – it's out Cumnock way.'

'They're talking about getting the SOCOs – must be a new crime scene.'

Valentine reached for the radio and spoke into the

mouthpiece. 'Jim, it's Bob Valentine. What's the story with Ardinsh Farm?'

There was a gap on the line and then the desk sergeant replied, 'If you stayed away from that Krispy Kreme in Braehead you might be able to hear what's going over the radio, Bob.'

'You've spoiled the surprise. I have a dirty big doughnut sitting here for you.'

'Lovely. I might even get a chance to eat it before midnight.'

'So what's all the commotion?'

'Excavator driver's turned up an oil drum in one of the fields. Looks like an old corpse inside.'

'Old? How old?'

'Put it this way, it could pass for a pharaoh.'

Valentine altered his tone. 'No more jokes, Jim, please.'

'Who's joking? The corpse is mummified.'

2

As he replaced the radio receiver, Valentine gazed straight ahead. For a moment he said nothing, then exhaling loudly and pressing his back into the driver's seat, he turned to DS McCormack.

'Well, this could be a bit awkward.'

'What do you mean, sir?'

'Ardinsh Farm is – I mean was – Sandy Thompson's place. It was in the family for generations.'

'And why's that awkward for us?'

'Sandy's dead.'

'Oh . . .'

'No, I mean he's just died. I'm sure it's his funeral today.'

'And how do you know this?'

'Cumnock's a small town. I grew up there, remember.' McCormack's expression said she still needed convincing. 'And my father's going to Sandy's funeral . . . I'm bloody sure it's today. He was at the old spit and polish routine on his shoes when I left this morning.'

'Right, I see why that might be awkward for the ones left behind, trying to grieve.'

'No, it's not that . . . Look, we need to get going.'

Valentine put the car into gear and eased up the clutch.

As the Vectra met the main road he was already deep in thought. By the M77 the detective wore a troubled expression that meant his mind was absorbed in the possibilities of another murder investigation on Ayrshire soil.

It hadn't always been like this. Ayr had been a bustling market town as long as he could remember, but somewhere along the way it had changed. It seemed more like a small city than the town he had spent most of his career in. It seemed, too, to have inherited all the social ills and associated problems of its larger counterparts in Scotland's central belt.

His own stabbing, in no less a target than the heart, had come as a shock to the local force. His subsequent death on an emergency-room operating table, and then his revival with the help of more than fifty pints of blood, had been the talk of King Street station for months. No one quite knew how to process a senior officer being attacked by a drug dealer in this way; there were some in uniform who still treated him like a sort of hero. But Valentine knew it was no badge of honour. The scar – thick as a man's index finger – down his chest was not something he regarded with any degree of pride.

He was lucky to come home after that night, as his wife was fond of reminding him every time the job got too arduous – or dangerous. Clare wouldn't welcome the fact that he was starting on another murder investigation; neither would his two daughters. But this was his job; he knew nothing else, could do nothing else. The job was all he had known for the whole of his adult life, and perhaps even before.

As Valentine's car reached the outskirts of Cumnock, it

didn't feel like coming home – he could never quite call the place where he was raised home. This was the town where he watched his father battle on the picket lines with police waving fivers at the striking, starving miners. They'd burnt out their cars, the police, and no one travelled alone fearing reprisals for the never-ending violence. It was a war zone then, and for a time in his youth it was the distorted prism through which he viewed the entire world.

He knew he wanted to be a cop in those early years in Cumnock. Not because he idolised the police, or harboured the types of beliefs he read about in Batman comics, but because he wanted to live somewhere better. Valentine wanted to live in a world where people didn't behave like animals and brutes; he wanted to weed those out. He was a hunter, of sorts, only he didn't know that then.

'Is it far now?' said DS McCormack.

The sound of a human voice startled Valentine, broke his reverie and forced him to rewire his thinking to find a response. 'Erm, no, not far now at all.'

'What about the funeral, where's that being held?'

'I'm guessing it'll probably be in the town. I can't see it going farther afield. Sandy was on his own at the end.'

'And what type of a man was he?' McCormack managed to make her voice sound businesslike.

'He was a farmer, Sylvia. What does that say about him?'

'I just meant . . .'

The DI cut in. 'I know what you meant. He wasn't known to police, to use the common parlance. I didn't know him personally. We'd have nodded at each other in the Spar, y'know, but that was about it.'

'Nothing to indicate he might be involved in this sort of thing then?'

'What sort of thing? We haven't even reached the scene yet.'

'We know there's a body.'

'We know it's mummified too, if Jim's to be relied upon. But no, I wouldn't think Sandy Thompson knew much about the dark arts of ancient Egypt. Probably couldn't find the place on a map.'

'People bury things in the country, under the cover of darkness – might be nothing to do with him even though it's on his land.'

Valentine started to slow the car. 'Yes, in the absence of soon-to-be-cemented motorway flyovers, a nice secluded country spot seems to suit your average murderer with a corpse to dispose of quite nicely.'

The DI brought the car to a halt behind a white police Audi with no one inside. As the detectives got out of the Vectra and peered over the top of a drystone dyke Valentine pointed to the white tent, surrounded by white-suited figures and uniformed officers. 'Ally and Phil must be inside,' said Valentine.

'Must be, sir.'

The DI tried to open a gate that separated the road from the field, but it wouldn't budge. 'It's locked. We'll just have to shimmy over it.'

'I can shimmy well enough, boss.'

In the long, wet grass of the field the officers trudged towards the tent. The ground was hard-packed but remained beset by occasional squelchy patches underfoot.

DS McCormack was the first to break the silence. 'I'm

thinking, if Sandy Thompson just died, then how did the farm get sold off so quickly?'

'Good question. Sandy would never sell whilst he was alive . . . and I heard of a few offers.'

'So there must be family.'

'No, there's not. His wife died years ago, 1980 or something. They never had any kids except for the boy they took in, Garry.'

'Was he adopted?'

'I don't think so. He was fostered for a bit from the boy's home, Columba House. Look, you can see it over there.' Valentine raised his arm and extended a finger towards a large grey building on the edge of the low-lying moorland. It looked like it might once have been a hunting lodge but had fallen into disrepair. Large damp patches were exposed beneath the breaks in the seventies roughcasting, some windows had been boarded up and those that hadn't been covered were smashed or cracked.

'What a creepy old building.'

'It was a very strange place. I remember the boys they had there said they were from broken homes. I don't suppose that's a phrase we use nowadays.'

'It doesn't sound very PC.'

Valentine smirked. 'I suppose not. They were all quiet kids when they came to the school. Silent some of them, like they were living in terror of authority. In the playground they were totally different – rough as bloody guts they were.'

DS McCormack stopped still. 'So this Garry, he must have copped for the lot.'

'The farm? I doubt it. I'm not sure he was that integrated

18

into the Thompson family. He worked the farm for a few years after Sandy went downhill, but it never lasted. I wouldn't be surprised if the old boy had sold it on the fly to some profiteer on the basis that once he'd popped his clogs they can bring in the bulldozers.'

'You know how that sounds, boss?' McCormack hadn't started to walk again.

'I do.' Valentine halted, turning round to face the DS. 'I do, Sylvia. It sounds like we might need to consider doing a post-mortem on Sandy Thompson, but I'm not keen to march into his funeral today and tell them we're putting the anchors on their wee ceremony, are you?'

'Not really, sir.'

'So let's see where we are.' He indicated the white tent. 'Or more accurately, where Ally and Phil have got to. With any luck there's a sound explanation for why the contractors are so keen to get started that they couldn't wait until the day *after* Sandy's funeral.'

3

The closer they got to the white tent which had been erected by the SOCOs, the louder the stray canvas straps flapping in the wind sounded. There was a full-height doorway in the tent, a long roll of canvas attached with straps at the top where the noise came from, and inside hung a fly screen. The screen seemed wholly unnecessary to Valentine in this weather, unless its purpose was to keep out the incessant drizzle.

The detectives reached the opening and peered inside. It was Valentine who noticed Chief Superintendent Marion Martin first, but it was McCormack who commented.

'The super's here.'

'What's she playing at now?'

McCormack straightened herself, leaned back from the flapping tent. 'You know Dino, boss.' The remark was supposed to be sufficiently vague as to attest to the CS's niggling manner.

'She'll be playing the hands-on card. I can't stand it when she's like that – everything takes twice as long to get done.'

'And logic goes out the window.'

'You noticed that too?'

'I noticed that she tends to focus on the end rather than the means.'

'You're being too polite. What you mean to say is she wants results without graft, wants her crime stats to be the top consideration. Well, it doesn't work like that, Sylvia.'

'No need to preach to the choir, boss.'

DI Valentine removed his hands from his coat pockets and turned to face the tent. He prised the Velcro fastening free and forced his way through the new opening. DS McAlister was the first to acknowledge the officers.

'Hello, boss,' said Ally, breaking off his gaze to direct a nod in McCormack's direction. He handed the officers two boxes, one with latex gloves protruding from the top and the other blue shoe covers. They mechanically snapped out the contents and put them in place.

'What have you got for us, Ally?' said Valentine.

Before the DS had a chance to answer, the chief super opened into a yell. 'Bob, over here!'

Valentine exchanged glances with McAlister, who was already raising his eyebrows towards the tent's roof.

As he approached the CS, Valentine took in the scene. It was cramped in the tent; even with only two more officers arriving the place was now being negotiated in shuffles and halted steps. Two SOCOs, dressed head to toe in white, were peering over the edge of an excavation hole in the ground. There appeared to be a large object inside but it was too dark beneath the canvas to see clearly what it might be. The closer he got to the hole, the stronger the stench became. It was an unusual smell, not like the decaying flesh he associated with crime scenes – far mustier, almost spicy; one his late mother would have called fusty.

'Well, what's the story with the Thin Man?' said CS Martin.

Valentine was a little taken aback by the query, until it registered who was making it. 'Case closed as far as I'm concerned.'

'Oh, shit . . . natural causes?'

The DI wasn't sure how to take Martin's remark. Was she seriously disappointed that another human being hadn't met their end in a suspicious manner? Because the alternative was that she was favouring murder.

'Cancer – he was riddled with it.'

'Can we ID him now?'

'No. We haven't a clue who he is. He's not from the British Isles if the clothes and reports of his accent are anything to go by. I wouldn't expect a result there either. He clearly didn't want to be found; must have had his reasons.'

'Yes, well, we have our reasons for wanting to identify him.'

Valentine knew just what those reasons were, as far as the chief super was concerned. She wanted to see her force on the television again; she wanted the plaudits for solving the case that had attracted the public's attention in such an unprecedented way. It was capitalising on the publicity the case had generated in the most obvious manner.

'You know as well as I do that some cases are simply not solvable.'

'We have enough cold cases piled up in that basement to sink a battleship, Bob.'

'One more unsolved mystery won't make any difference then. Look, can we move on? If you want the proof that

22

crime never sleeps . . .' He waved a hand in the direction of the ground.

CS Martin inwardly fumed. 'It's the body of a minor.'

'We're in Cumnock, be careful with your pronunciation.'

'Not that type of miner – though this one did come out the ground.'

Valentine scanned the scene quickly. 'I take it the doc has been and gone in his usual hyper-efficient manner?'

'To be fair to him, he didn't have to do much more than glance inside the oil drum.'

Valentine crouched down towards the hole. He could see the rim of the steel barrel protruding above the earth; long scraping streaks, like teeth marks, had exposed the metal. A steel lid that had obviously once been attached lay at the foot of the drum. Valentine eyed the excavator tracks that sat either side of the hole and assessed that a protruding arm from the digger outside had caused the damage.

As he got closer to the hole, he leaned on the rim of the drum and peered inside.

'Here,' said CS Martin. 'You'll need this.' She handed him a thin pen torch.

Valentine shone the torch's beam into the barrel and flinched. A screaming pain entered the base of his skull and nausea washed over him. He thought he might vomit, but he steadied his grip on the rim of the drum and continued.

In the light's beam he could see two small hands, bony and black, like they were covered in leather. The hands were cable-tied and rested on the crown of a small head, too small to be a man's. The figure looked to be in prayer.

Valentine spoke: 'Ally, was that the fiscal depute I saw out there?'

'Yes, boss. He was a bit, how can I put it? Shaken up, even for Colin Scott.'

The DI rose. 'I can't fault a man for that. Jim Prentice wasn't kidding when he said the corpse was mummified.'

'Horrific, isn't it?' said CS Martin.

'I've never seen anything like it in my entire career. Those hands . . . you can still see the flesh. It's like they've been frozen that way since the time of death.'

'The drum was sealed, sir,' said Ally. 'The doc reckoned all the moisture had been locked out, effectively preserving the contents.'

Valentine faced the team. He was pulling the latex gloves from his hands when he spoke. 'Right, if the fiscal and the medic have seen this then I want the barrel removed from the ground and the contents examined.'

'Yes, sir,' said Ally.

'I want this forensic team doubled and the contents photographed and catalogued within the hour. Phil, get on to Wrighty. I want him to look at this today – no excuses – and if it's not his thing, then he gets someone in – today!'

'Yes, boss.'

'We have a dead child, and a crime scene that has been remarkably well kept for us. If we can't get a jump on this case through the boffins, then I don't know when they'll ever be of use to us.' Valentine rubbed the back of his head; the dull pain had become an ache now.

'Boss, what about door to door?' said DS Donnelly. 'There's a farmhouse up there, I saw a for-sale sign, but . . .'

The DI cut in. 'No. Leave that for now. Any witnesses and suspects are likely to be long gone, or in need of very good memories. Did the doc say how long he'd been in there?'

'No, though he did say at least twenty-five years.'

'That's what I was worried about. Hopefully there'll be some more evidence in the barrel. If it's preserved as well as the corpse then we might be lucky and find the poor lad's bus pass or dinner ticket. Get it all looked at. And, Phil, don't be a stranger to the phone. I want calls with every step of the way.'

'Yes, boss.'

'Do we know who owns the property?'

DS Donnelly removed a sheaf of paper from beneath his clipboard. 'The site manager gave me this.'

Valentine took the sheet of A4. 'Blairgowan Construction. They're not local.'

'No, Glasgow, sir. And they've been about as helpful and accommodating as you'd expect them to be.'

'Perhaps someone should tell them it's not a pair of nesting barn owls we're dealing with, it's murder . . . Hang on, this is a title deed, and it says they purchased the land and buildings in October of 2014.'

'From a Mr Keirns, I think it says.'

'It does indeed. Our very own Mr Garry Keirns.' Valentine headed out of the tent. 'Sylvia, you're with me.'

'Are we going where I think we are, sir?'

The DI was marching through the wet grass towards the car. 'If you think we're going to interrupt a funeral, then yes.'

McCormack stopped still. 'I knew you were going to say that. I was hoping you wouldn't, but I knew it.'

4

'Hang on a minute, boss. Shouldn't we wait to see what comes out of the barrel?' said DS McCormack.

'I think we can trust Phil and Ally with that. Besides, it looks like the construction crew have knocked off, and they'll need to call back the digger operator to get it out of there. We haven't got the time to waste if we want to bring in Keirns.'

The detective hadn't altered his stride. He was at the gate now, climbing over the rail on his way back to the car. McCormack gritted her teeth and followed him over the top.

Inside the car, McCormack spoke up again: 'So we're really going to do this?'

'Interrupt the funeral, you mean? I can't see any other way.'

'We could secure the scene, sir, supervise the removal of the oil drum.'

'And send in the Chuckle Brothers? I don't think so. This requires tact, Sylvia. They're good cops but neither have that particular talent.'

'I just thought . . .'

'I know what you thought.' Valentine proceeded to rub

the back of his head again. 'But we have to do our own dirty work this time.'

'Something the matter with your head?'

The DI jerked his hand away and started the car. 'Twisted a muscle or something.'

'OK.'

Valentine knew exactly what McCormack's response really said but resisted the urge to explain himself. He'd have enough of that to do later, when he got home to Clare and his father. The consequences of what he was about to do didn't sit easily with him, but he'd sooner be in full control than delegate it and have even more to explain in time.

The road to Cumnock Congregational Church wasn't long. Fields and moorland butted the road on either side whilst a light smirr pattered on the windscreen. It was familiar territory to the detective, but after what he had just seen, it felt like he was viewing the place with fresh eyes.

Valentine knew the streets he grew up in well, possibly even better than the streets of Ayr that he now walked daily. But the Cumnock of his boyhood appeared to him as another place entirely these days.

He calculated the child in the oil drum to be about ten years old, maybe a little older. If he'd been in the ground for twenty-five years like the doctor had guessed, that meant he was murdered when Valentine was in his early teens. It never occurred to him that this meant it might well have been him in the barrel – the ages were close enough, and murder was a random enough crime – because his thoughts were on the victim. A child had been murdered; there could hardly be a worse offence.

Children he'd gone to school with, played football with,

gone to the pictures with, could it be one of them? He saw their faces, the grey school jumpers, the old Bukta tracksuits they wore then, parkas, Clark's Commandos. They were all so alike; hardly a detail separated them.

They'd gone to Cubs together – Scouts too. School trips – that sailing holiday in Whiting Bay – those memories were sullied now. One of the boys, one he'd possibly known, had been murdered, and the killer might as well have left his tracks all over his doorstep. It all felt too close to home, too personal, but he knew if he was to catch this killer he'd have to push those thoughts aside. He had to keep an open mind, a focussed curiosity, because anything less was letting a child murderer go free.

They were entering the township when DS McCormack spoke again. 'This must all feel very strange for you, sir?'

'How do you mean?'

'Well, you grew up here. I can't imagine what that must be like.'

'You grew up in Glasgow. You worked there. I'm sure you had cases that felt close to home.'

'Glasgow's a big city – it's not the same. These places are claustrophobic – everybody knows everybody's business.'

'I wouldn't be so sure about that. And I wouldn't be relying on local gossip to be of any help to you. Cumnock's a law unto itself, after what they went through with the miners' strike people aren't keen to rat on their neighbour. And talking to the police is still cautiously frowned upon.'

'They're a bit backward at coming forward where I come from too. Nobody likes us; I'm well used to that.'

The church was built from picturesque red sandstone in a gothic, turreted style with an ornamental bell tower as the focal point. The cross on top of the tower was small, looked almost like an afterthought, but the stained-glass windows were vast, taking up a whole third of the main-facing wall.

Valentine headed for the entrance, aiming to park in the church grounds, but thought better of it and pulled up beyond the wrought-iron railings with two wheels on the pavement.

'Inside the grounds is for the family,' he said.

McCormack shrugged, her expression saying that she thought he was being unnecessarily pedantic. 'We're here to disrupt the occasion not join in.'

'I know. But some things just don't feel right.'

As they parked, a navy Range Rover exiting the church-yard caught Valentine's attention. Whoever was in the back was important enough to have a driver and kit him out with a uniform.

'Who's that?' said McCormack.

'Search me. I don't know anyone from Cumnock with a Range Rover, never mind a driver with a peaked cap.'

As the car passed, the detectives stared into the back window, which had been tinted but was clear enough to show the full-leather interior and a familiar face.

'I know him,' said McCormack. 'Isn't he that politician?'

Valentine nodded, watching the Range Rover speed away. '*Was* a politician – he's not any more. It's Gerald Fallon, and he used to be the sitting MP for Carrick, Cumnock and Doon Valley.'

'I know his face.'

'He was never off the telly for about twenty years. I think he was the longest sitting MP in Scotland. Seemed to do bloody well out of it anyway.'

'Did you catch the private plate?'

'GF 111 – must have cost almost as much as the car.'

'He probably got them both on expenses, before the row broke.'

Valentine grinned. 'Wouldn't surprise me. What I do find surprising is what the hell Gerry Fallon is doing at Sandy's funeral. I can't imagine they were old muckers.'

As they started for the church Valentine began to vigorously rub the back of his head once again.

'Sure that's muscle strain?' said McCormack.

The DI snatched away his hand. 'Let's get inside. If you spot my old man, give me the nod.'

'Is that the plan, expose your dad to as much embarrassment as possible?'

Valentine paused, weighing the detective's words. 'He knows these people, knows Keirns. I'm going to ask my dad to point him out. Hopefully we can do this with a minimal fuss.'

McCormack looked at her watch then back towards the church. 'The day's getting on. If we're lucky we might get them as they're coming out.'

'We'll see. If we can do it with the least disruption then all to the good.'

The police officers headed down the path for the church entrance, the sound of their shoes echoing on the flagstones.

'Sir, can I ask about Keirns?' said McCormack.

'I'm not sure there's much I can tell you. He was at Columba House, that much you already know.'

'That was the big old building, next to the farm. The one that's all boarded up now?'

Valentine nodded as he walked. 'It used to be a reformatory for boys in Victorian times. I think they called it an approved school or something when I was a kid. It's always been one of these places for wayward kids, boys waiting in custody and so on. I don't know that much about it, except that it closed at the end of the eighties, some scandal involving the staff and the boys.'

'Child abuse?'

'Something like that. I don't know the details.'

'But would Keirns have been there then?'

Valentine had reached the door. He gripped the oversized handle. 'I suppose he must have left by then. But not by long.'

The vestibule was tiled, a broad mosaic in mostly terracotta, greens and blacks. Every tile had a chip or a crack; some were missing altogether. Damp coats hung steaming on old hat pegs, whilst wet umbrellas stood in the stand and clung to the window ledge. Beyond the heavy oak doors came the sound of dour preaching in a west of Scotland accent. Occasional coughs broke in-between the gaps in the speech.

'OK, come on, what's the worst that can happen?' said Valentine.

'Well, the place could come down on us for a start.'

'You're not making this any easier.'

'I'm just saying . . .'

'Well, don't.'

5

Valentine's father wasn't hard to spot, being tall and gaunt, stooping slightly above the others with their hymn books out. He didn't seem to notice the officers at first and kept singing, but when they reached his pew and started to crab crawl their way towards him he appeared perplexed.

'Is it the girls, Bob?' he whispered.

'What?'

'Has there been an accident?'

'No, Dad. Nothing like that.'

A shuffle of bodies indicated the end of the hymn; a few glanced at Valentine and McCormack.

'Dad, we're here on police business.'

'I don't understand.'

'I don't have the time to explain.' Valentine felt conscious of causing a stir. He looked to the front and tried to blend.

'Surely it's nothing to do with Sandy's burial.'

'No, it's nothing to do with that. Well, it is and it isn't . . . look, which one down there is Garry Keirns?'

'Garry Keirns.' His voice came at the normal volume and caused a woman in a bobble hat from the row in front to turn around.

Valentine's father lowered his tone. 'Why do you want Garry?'

'Which one is he?'

The old man pointed to a seated figure at the end of the front row. He was close to fifty years old with greying red hair that covered his collar. Valentine noticed he wasn't wearing a suit like the others seated nearby, but jeans and a tired-looking anorak.

'The one in the pale-grey jacket?' said Valentine.

'That's him, yes.' His father placed a hand on Valentine's arm. 'Please, Bob, don't interrupt the ceremony. Let them get Sandy in the ground first.'

'Dad, I have a job to do.'

'These are your people too, son.'

'If you'd just seen what I have, that wouldn't count for much.'

'Whatever your reasons, let them grieve. A family has a right to bury its dead.'

The congregation rose again. The pall-bearers were surrounding the coffin.

'OK, Dad. But after that we'll have to move. I'm not here to embarrass you.'

'You have your job to do – I'm quite sure you've weighed the consequences.'

His father's pale eyes gazed at him for a moment and then he got up to follow the others into the churchyard.

Valentine rose to follow him but was held back by DS McCormack. 'You might be better putting a bit of distance between you.'

'I think I've already done that.'

As the detective moved off he felt McCormack grip

his arm again. 'Seriously, you should hang back, give him some space.'

'You think that'll spare his blushes?'

She shrugged. 'It might, a little.'

'Sylvia, you don't know Cumnock. I'm already the talk of the steamie just for being here. I knew that the second I walked through the door.'

The crowd followed the pall-bearers and the coffin to a prepared piece of ground in the graveyard. Two men stood under a bare elm, shovels propped behind them on the tree's bole, waiting to bury the deceased's remains. As the minister made his dour chants, the sky seemed to clear and weak sunlight broke the clouds. It was a temporary affair, however, and by the time the coffin had been lowered and the first sod cast, the grey wash had returned.

Valentine and McCormack stood a respectful distance away, behind an elderly lady who dabbed her eyes with a white handkerchief and a bull-necked man who accompanied her, supporting her elbow with both hands.

When the gathering started to disperse, Valentine felt a surge of panic in his chest that he might lose sight of Keirns, and then he spotted him and jogged down the crowd's flank, against the flow of movement. All eyes followed him, and at the end he met his father, who was shaking his head at the mild commotion.

'Your mother would have been ashamed of you.'

Valentine had no words to reply with. He gazed at his father for a moment and then he was reminded of his duty and sidestepped him on the way to Keirns.

DS McCormack followed, briskly pushing through. The pair stopped Keirns, blocking his path.

'What's all this?' said Keirns.

Warrant cards were produced. 'Are you Garry Keirns?'

'Yes, I am. What's going on?'

'I'm Detective Inspector Bob Valentine and this is DS Sylvia McCormack. We have some questions we'd like to ask you.'

Keirns removed his hands from his pockets and showed open palms. 'At my foster father's funeral?'

'I'm sorry for the inconvenience,' said Valentine. He was dully aware of a halt in the proceedings as the few remaining attendees took in the spectacle.

'Did you hear what I said?'

'We'd really like to conduct this in a civilised manner, Mr Keirns,' said Valentine. He motioned him towards the path. 'If you'd like to accompany me to the station.'

'The station!' Keirns snapped. 'Am I under arrest?'

'No, sir. You're not under arrest.'

'Well, you can't bloody well touch me then. I'm going nowhere.' He barged past the officers.

Valentine caught Keirns's coat sleeve and pulled him back. 'I'm conducting a murder investigation.'

'*What*? Murder.' His voice rose to an unnatural pitch; his words seemed to startle the motionless crowd into action, and the minister encouraged them to move on.

'We've found a body out at Ardinsh Farm. I don't think this is the place to go into details, do you?'

Keirns was silent. He looked like a man whose thought process had shut down. He started to tug at the sagging black knot of tie around his neck.

DS McCormack encouraged him down the path, towards the car. 'If you'd like to accompany us to the station now, Mr Keirns.'

'I . . . I don't know anything about a murder.' His face was bereft of emotion; even when he spoke his lips hardly seemed to move.

'We can talk about that at the police station, Mr Keirns,' said McCormack.

As they went Valentine looked out for his father but couldn't see him. He had never known his father to react so cruelly, and his harsh words played over now. He knew there was no apology or explanation that could fix things. It had already gone beyond the point where words might help balm the wound.

At the car Valentine felt a sudden sharpness in the back of his head, like he'd been smacked with a broom handle. The pain was short-lived, fleeting, but enough to halt him mid-stride.

'What is it?' said McCormack.

'Nothing.' Valentine continued towards the vehicle and placed a hand on Keirns's shoulder. 'I'll take him from here.'

'Please, don't do that thing,' said Keirns. 'With the hand on my crown as I get in the car. I see that on the telly all the time. It always makes them look guilty.'

Valentine removed his hand from Keirns's shoulder and took a step back.

'Thank you,' said Keirns. 'I just think, y'know, they've seen enough today already.'

Valentine closed the car door behind Keirns and moved to the driver's seat. As he was stepping inside, his mobile rang out.

'Yes, Valentine.'

'Hello, boss.'

'Phil, what's up?'

'Well, there's good and bad news, sir. You said you wanted it all, didn't you?'

Valentine perched his shoe on the car's door sill. 'Go on.'

'We got the oil drum out, an old ICI number with unusual markings, but I doubt a trace on it will do us much good. It's likely just been a convenient size and shape.'

'And the contents? Tell me the body is on its way to Wrighty.'

'I'm coming to that. It weighed a ton, sir. It was weighted down with rocks, big ones, and some smashed-up slabs.'

'Makes you think it wasn't intended for the ground – sounds like it was going overboard.'

'We needed to use the JCB to get it out the muck. I wouldn't have thought it moveable without that. Anyway, the boy's body came out easier, and it's gone up to pathology in Glasgow. But we have another problem now.'

Valentine watched DS McCormack get out of the car and approach him; she appeared to sense something. 'What is it?'

The DI flagged her down. 'Go on then, Phil, what did you pull out of the barrel?'

'We haven't pulled anything else out of there yet. You see, we had to call back the doc and the fiscal . . .'

'What are you saying?'

'There's a second body in there.'

Valentine lowered the mobile and glanced in the car; Garry Keirns was gesturing for them to get going.

'Boss, what's up?' said McCormack.

Valentine's voice was a confused rasp. 'We have another body.'

6

May 1982

I'm still hungry but not so cold now. Mammy used to say I was always hungry, that it must be the hollow legs I had. I miss those things she said.

The bus carriage rattles on the bumpy road. I've no idea where we are or why I'm sat up at the back by myself with the horsehair from the burst chair poking at my bare legs. Shorts – what manner of dress is that for a boy of my age? I'm nine and haven't worn shorts for years – at least two anyway.

The man with a nose like a hawk keeps turning round to look at me. He takes a quick glance, without so much as a smile, and then turns back to the driver. They talk about the football like it's a subject for grown-ups only, but I know about the World Cup.

I want to say about the lad Rossi who plays for Italy, how he always scores the winner. I want to say about the Polish players, Boniek and Lato, the deadliest strikers in the finals. And I want to say about Norman Whiteside, the Irish lad from the north, who was only seventeen when he pulled on the green jersey for the first time.

Mammy was Irish, the man with the hawk nose told me. He said it made me the stock of navvies and whores and then he said he'd call me Taff because of my name. Donal Welsh is my name, but I don't think I'm really Welsh at all.

The coach leaves the road and starts up an even bumpier one. I thought the first road meant we were in the country, but now I see it only meant we were on our way to the country. This is the country; the branches of the trees scrape the windows as we go by the bright green fields.

The beak told me I was going to be sent here. He had a name for the place, a fancy one, but I wasn't listening. I find it hard to pay much attention to grown-ups when they're giving out at me. I switch off; that's what they say anyway.

That was after the hospital. I don't know how I got there, not really anyway. But I remember Mammy had passed by then. It was me that found her with the needle in her arm at the squat. I told a grown-up there but he only swore and left. I think he was Mammy's boyfriend.

In the hospital they had a needle in me too, in my hand though, feeding me they said. They sheared off my hair too. I don't know why they would do that. I remember the hospital well. I loved the tight white sheets, the smell of the soap on them, and the feeds they gave you. Sometimes I had custard. I didn't want to leave but they made me.

'The boy is a delinquent,' the woman said. She was talking to the beak, but I don't know who she was. 'By any definition of the word.'

'Is it your opinion that the boy is in danger of criminality?' said the beak.

'It's not a matter of opinion; it's a matter of fact. The boy has already engaged in criminality. Would you like my colleague to expound?'

'If you consider it useful.'

That's when the Old Gannet read from his notebook; they called him that because he used to take scoops off your plate if you didn't eat fast enough. He didn't need the food, the size of the belly on him, but he took it to be a bastard.

' . . . And that, your honour, is when the assault occurred, occasioning the cut above my left eye, which required stitching at the hospital.'

He'd asked for it. How was I to know the plate would break? I wouldn't do it again, not after the bruising I got. No, sir. I wouldn't repeat that mistake twice.

'Are charges pending?' said the beak.

'No charges have been placed.'

'And is it your opinion the boy could make use of normal community facilities?'

'Not immediately. In time he could attend school. We are confident enough that he has some faculties.'

'Very well. Your charge is to be placed in a community school deemed suitable by the local authority, preferably an agricultural colony where he can work off any excess energies prior to eventual schooling.'

'The authority has a place in mind that might just fit the bill.'

The coach struggled over the hill, the engine wheezing, and all the colours changed. The grass was still as green

40

as can be – that would be with the rain – but the sky was grey now, some purple clouds blackening at their edges. Out the window looked like the kind of picture you'd see in old movies about werewolves or Frankenstein and the like. I didn't like the look of it – not one little bit. I didn't want to be here at all.

7

DI Bob Valentine sat in his office and stared out of the window. The sky was its usual overcast shade of gunmetal, with a pink smear along the horizon. The commuter traffic was building on the King Street roundabout, and the sound of impatient drivers blaring horns echoed all the way from the town centre. It was a picture of normalcy he knew the town of Ayr usually occupied, but somehow nothing was as he had once known it.

Something drew Valentine from his chair and he approached the large window, staring further into the scene he knew so well. A ship was docked in the harbour, an unusual sight at the best of times, but the tall, elegant vessel spoke of simpler days. It would be a tourist ship, some kids on an adventure outing perhaps; he'd read about it in the *Post* eventually.

His thoughts were drifting again, to hopes the kids on the ship were being looked after. It was an adult's responsibility, to care for children. It was every adult's responsibility. Children were the most precious gift we had. They were everything – our joy, our pleasure, the very symbol of our love. Children were to be treasured. He thought of Clare and the girls. And he thought of two children, unknown to him, with their hands cable-tied, crammed into a rusty oil drum.

When he had first looked at the child in the barrel, with the blackened, leathered face, he wanted to take away his pain. It was an overwhelming feeling – a need like a parent's to keep a child safe. He didn't know who the child was, and it didn't matter, because he was every child. He was the child Valentine had once been, who played on the same streets, collected conkers and ran errands for adults, set jam jars out for bees in summer and made snowmen in winter. The child was his friend, every one of his friends, climbing trees and kicking a football at a wall, playing soldiers with sticks and knock door run. And then it hit him. At some point, all those long summers and longer winters ended for two children. There were two fewer children queuing at the ice-cream van when it did the rounds. Two fewer children being called in by their mothers as the sun faded and playtime drew to a close. For no reason that those children could have fathomed, everything ended. The lives they had known, the hopes they had held, any dreams for the future, ended.

Child murder was the most grievous sin Valentine could imagine. Taking one child away from their family was a crime like no other; but worse, it diminished us all. Child murder took all our futures away and told us there was nothing left. Because if we couldn't care for our children, couldn't protect their lives, we had nothing left. And we deserved nothing more.

Valentine closed his eyes and rested his forehead on the windowpane. The glass was cold and damp, and he felt his skin absorbing the moisture. His head felt warm. There was still an ache in the back of his skull that he couldn't account for, but that pain didn't matter to him now. It was the feeling of sadness, of a solemn loss, that had overtaken everything else; he was filled with hurts that were greater than himself.

The hand that touched his forearm felt very far away, and it took several seconds for him to register what it was.

'Boss, are you ready?' said DS McCormack.

Valentine snapped out of his thoughts and stepped away from the window, wiping his forehead with the back of his hand. 'Sorry, Sylvia, I was off on one.'

'Sir?'

She deserved an explanation, as much as he could supply anyway. 'Those kiddies, I was thinking about them. I don't think I'll ever shake that boy's image from my head.'

'Me neither. It's horrifying. Are you sure you're OK now?'

'I won't lie to you – I don't feel myself. You of all people know how I get, since the . . .' He touched the centre of his chest with fingertips.

'You don't feel yourself?'

Valentine looked back to the window. 'Do you remember what that bloke said?'

'You mean Crosbie?'

'Yeah, him. He told me, in time, I'd come to know what the signs were. That I'd get to know when they were coming.'

'Is that where you think you are now?'

He shook his head. 'I don't know. I know something's not right with me. I feel this impending dread inside me, but I've no idea what it is or what it means.'

'You really should see Crosbie again. I'll set something up as soon as I can.'

'Now wait a minute.'

'Sir, this could be related to the case. All those other times it happened . . . just think how much easier it would be if you could control this for your benefit.'

'I don't know, Sylvia.'

'You have trouble buying into all of this, I get that, but didn't Crosbie say you were over-intellectualising?'

'I don't think that's a word he would use.'

'You know what I mean. He said you were trying to comprehend something in your mind that couldn't be understood at the level of the mind.'

'Yes. Something like that.'

'Your trouble isn't a problem you can rationalise, Bob. You need to find acceptance. I can't do that for you.'

'OK then.'

DS McCormack turned for the door; her movements indicated the conversation was over. 'Are you ready for Keirns now?'

'As ready as I'll ever be.'

Garry Keirns sat facing the two officers with his hands positioned flatly in front of him. They were not big hands, certainly not farmer's hands, but small and almost podgy. The nails had been bitten to the quick and the knuckles were freckled. Thin wisps of red hair occupied the extremities and joined with more freckles where they attached to the wrists. As confidently as Keirns had laid out his hands, when he caught the officers assessing them, he whipped them away and put them beneath the tabletop.

'Bit jumpy aren't you, Garry?' said Valentine.

'I don't think so. No more than anyone in my position would be.'

'And what position's that?'

He huffed. 'Do I need to spell it out? Jesus, you raided my foster father's funeral not an hour ago.'

DS McCormack replied, 'I think that might be an over-statement of the facts, Garry.'

He shook his head. 'Look, just get on with it. What the hell do you want from me?'

Valentine detailed the morning's events, adding the second body at the end of his description of the first. When he was finished speaking Keirns sat impassively before them as if he was preparing himself for further shocks to come. It was difficult for the DI to judge his reaction because there was little or no reaction at all. He had often found that, in similar circumstances, people simply shut out the fantastic because they had no points of reference for it.

'Have you nothing to say, Garry?'

A grey tongue touched his dry lips. 'Well, no, not really.' He paused, moving his head slightly to the side but keeping his gaze on the officers. 'To tell you the truth, I'm a bit flabbergasted.'

'It's a lot to absorb,' said McCormack. 'Take your time.'

'I don't mean that,' he snapped. 'I mean I'm bloody stunned you got me in here thinking I'd have anything to do with putting young ones in a barrel, sealing it up and burying it in the ground. Do I look like an idiot?'

Valentine shifted in his seat; he was aware of McCormack regarding his reaction. 'If you don't mind me saying,

46

Mr Keirns, that's a very callous response to the news I've just given you.'

Keirns leaned forward, jutting out of his chair. He showed his hands again; this time he was pointing fingers. 'Don't try and twist this.'

'We're not in the business of twisting things,' said McCormack. 'The point the detective inspector is trying to make is that the bodies of two children have been recovered from your former property today and your main point of attention seems to be on your own grievance.'

The fingers were retracted; he patted the tabletop whilst he spoke. 'I'm not saying that, of course it's very sad. I feel for the families, I really do, but it is nothing whatsoever to do with me. Now do you get that bit? Nothing to do with me.'

'I think we understand what you're saying,' said the DI.

'Grand.' Keirns rose from the table and moved away from it. 'Then can I go now?'

'You're not under arrest, Mr Keirns; you're free to leave at your own choosing. But there are one or two aspects we'd like you to clarify for us.'

Keirns stepped back to the table and eased the chair out once more. As he sat down Valentine removed a sheaf of paper and presented it to him.

'What's this?'

'I believe it's what you call a deed of sale. Or should I say, a photocopy.'

'Yes, well, what of it?'

'Can I draw your attention to the date of the exchange of contracts, Mr Keirns?'

He rustled the paper in exaggerated fashion. 'It says . . . 2014.'

'But Sandy Thompson only passed away last week.'

'That's right.'

'How did you acquire the deeds to his property as far back as 2014 then?'

Keirns pushed away the paper. 'What has this got to do with anything?'

DS McCormack addressed Keirns. 'We're merely trying to establish the facts surrounding ownership of the crime scene. This is standard practice, sir.'

He inflated his cheeks and ran his small fingers through his hair. 'Look, I . . . I . . . Sandy was like a father to me and, well, when he started to get on, he had nobody. I didn't pressurise him to give me the farm in any way if that's what you're getting at.'

'No one is suggesting anything of the sort,' said McCormack.

'The farm hadn't been paying its way for a long time. Jesus, Sandy was winding the place down when I started labouring there in the eighties.'

'Winding down?' said Valentine.

'The farm had been around for generations, had been big, much bigger, but land got sold along the way – not just by Sandy but before him. It was all tied up with the Columba House folk too. That's what kept it going longer than it should have been a working farm.'

'Columba House has been closed for years.'

'Yeah, it was 1989 or something they shut up.'

'There was an investigation at the time.'

'I was long gone from the place by then.'

Valentine removed the piece of paper and quietly inserted it back in the blue folder it had came from.

'You were one of the Columba House boys?'

'Yes. I was, for my sins.'

'What sins were they?'

'It's a figure of speech.'

'What dates were you there, Mr Keirns?'

'I don't know. I was a kid; late seventies to eighty-two I think I started at the farm. They'll have records you can check. I've nothing to hide.'

'From 1982 to 2014 is a long time to work a farm that was, as you say, winding down.'

'We got by. I was mainly Sandy's carer by the time Columba closed. Look, is this questioning going anywhere? I'm getting a bit tired of it now.'

'We're nearly finished. I just wanted to ask you about this unusual deal you struck with Blairgowan Construction. How did it come about?'

'They wanted the land, they approached me.'

'What did they want the land for?'

'Posh houses and a new road – can't you ask them?'

'And they were happy to wait till Sandy passed away?'

'They didn't want the property to go somewhere else, I guess. It suited us, it suited Sandy – he got to stay there right to the end. Is that everything?'

'Just one more, Mr Keirns: where are you living now?'

'Ayr. I live in Ayr.'

Valentine stood up and collected his folder. 'Give your address to DS McCormack please. We'll be in touch, so I'd appreciate it if you let us know your movements, especially if you intend to leave town.'

8

DI Valentine's office looked on to the main incident room. It was little more than a glassed-off corner of the bigger area, and he often referred to it as the conservatory in mocking terms. He did, however, have the consolation of the large windows that overlooked the car park and the broader sweep of King Street towards the roundabout. The office's positioning also afforded the DI the ability to keep track of his team, who seemed to be returning to the station in greater numbers now.

As Valentine stood in the corner of the window he eyed the goings of the car park. DS McCormack had taken Garry Keirns to the front desk herself but was returning as Valentine pointed out Keirns leaving the building.

'One of the funeral goers dropped off his car and left the keys with Jim. Not a bad car – a BMW,' said McCormack.

'Five series too; the three series obviously wasn't flash enough for him.'

'Not bad at all.'

'Especially for a man who has never held a proper job these last thirty-odd years.' The silver saloon pulled on to the roundabout and took the second exit. 'Where does he stay?'

McCormack turned the pages of her spiral-bound note-book. 'Inkerman Court. Do you know it?'

'Yeah. It's part of the yuppie development down the harbour.'

'He didn't say it was a flat, there's no floor number indicated.'

'No, Inkerman's the town houses. Nice too, over three levels.'

'Well, Garry Keirns hasn't done too badly for a boy from the wrong side of the tracks.' She put down her notebook and pressed her shoulder against the wall. 'What did you make of him?'

'I thought he protested too much.'

'I thought so too. For a man who didn't like our questions, his answers were very fulsome. You realise we've nothing to go on. I mean, he gave us nothing.'

Valentine turned away from the window and eased himself on to the ledge. 'This case goes back years. We've just started. If Keirns is hiding something it might take us a while to flush it out.'

'His police record doesn't indicate any high-end crime. There's a few cannabis possessions from years back but the biggest seizure was about £150.'

'Makes you wonder why the local bobby even bothered at all.'

'Maybe they thought Keirns deserved it, y'know, like he was known to them and they wanted to push it through the courts to teach him a lesson.'

'Sounds plausible. Actually, when I think about the uniforms down there, it sounds more than bloody likely. Here's a name for your notebook – Davie Purves. He was the beat bobby in Cumnock for donkey's years, retired now, but he still stays out that way. Give him a yell and see if he has any inside info on Garry Keirns.'

'Will do, sir. I take it you're looking for more than gossip then?'

'I'll take what's going, but if Davie knows there's more to Keirns than the record shows then check it out too. They look after their own down there, the cops, but Davie's a pretty straight shooter. He wouldn't stiff you with any nonsense.'

'OK, I'll give him a knock. I'll also pull Keirns's social-security stamps. He hasn't been surviving on thin air or a carer's handout all this time,' said McCormack.

'Good idea. And get on to the Columba House folk – see what files they have on him. Might be nothing, might turn out to be juicy if we're lucky.'

'OK. That's all noted, sir.'

'Oh, and Blairgowan too.'

'The construction firm?'

'Yes. See who approached whom. Something tells me Keirns is not revealing the bigger picture there. Cumnock's hardly the bloody Gold Coast, I don't see developers falling over each other to snap up available land.'

'Yes, boss.' McCormack had been writing it down in her notebook; when she closed it over she spotted DS Donnelly. 'Looks like Phil's back, sir.'

'Right, let's get the squad together round the board. See what we've got so far.'

Valentine was first through the door, moving to the centre of the room and clapping his hands together. A diffuse collection of bodies took note, putting down folders and telephone receivers and gravitating to the detective inspector. The volume levels dropped to the point where the hum of the photocopier and the squeal of chair castors was all that could be heard.

'OK, everyone, I'd like your attention please,' said Valentine. 'Phil, Ally, can we get you both round the board. Bring me what you have. It's time we were all on the same page.'

'Sir.'

Ally approached the board, shuffling glossy paper in his hands. He removed something small and metallic that he was holding in his teeth and started to pin photographs on the board. 'Got some pictures from the photog, sir.'

'This is before we moved the first body, right?' said Valentine.

'There's more to come; this was all that was sitting in the printer when I was passing.'

DS Donnelly stepped in, leaning round Ally and addressing the DI. 'Pathology has the first body, sir. Wrighty's waiting for the SOCOs to finish up before moving the second.'

'You mean it's not out the barrel yet?'

'There's a lot to be bagged, sir. I don't think the drum has even been examined yet.'

Valentine waved down Donnelly. 'OK, son, it's not our usual crime scene – we'll have to be patient. Fortunately the crime occurred twenty-five years ago. We're not under the stopwatch on this one.'

'The SOCOs are putting in a late one, sir. We should have an index of the evidence early doors.'

'Good. When you get it catalogued I want you to go over it with a microscope yourself. If there's a shirt button in that barrel I want to know if it's from Woolworths or Marks & Spencer, do you understand?'

'Loud and clear, boss.'

'And who's tracing the barrel with ICI on the side?'

DS McAlister raised his hand. 'There's quite a few markings, nothing immediately decipherable, boss, but if we can tie it to a manufacturing source or retail point then we'll know better.'

'Good. Don't drag your heels on that. With any luck it's exotic, or better yet, unique. I want to know how it ended up in Cumnock. It might be that it was just something close to hand that they grabbed for their own purposes – it was the right size, shape and so on – but it might lead us somewhere we might not otherwise have been looking. A perp's workplace or spot on a delivery route. Check it all out – thoroughly.'

'I'm on it, sir.'

Valentine folded his arms, then quickly unfolded them and started to walk among the group. He found it easier to concentrate on the move, like the motion freed up thoughts. 'I want you to get into that basement tomorrow too, Ally. Any cases of missing children in the cold-case files from twenty-five to thirty years ago that you can find down there then I want to know about it. You might need to do some digging, but it could give us something to go on. Are there any unresolved disappearances? Any serial killers or predatory paedophiles we do know about sighted in the area at this time? Check them out, and pay close attention to the detective's handwritten notes. The stuff you don't normally see on the crime reports can quite often yield interesting information.'

'I'll get to that too, boss.'

'And watch the cobwebs down there.'

'I'll take a feather duster, sir.'

The group sniggered at the image. Valentine continued to strut. 'And, Phil, I want you to get hold of all the case files and all the newspaper reports on the scandal at Columba House.'

'Scandal, sir?' said Donnelly.

'It was a boys' home, of course there was a scandal. They shut the place in '89 after an investigation. You'll need to go to the archives, but Colleen in the media unit might help you with the newspaper cuttings, if you talk nicely to her, that is.'

'I think I can manage that.'

'Oh, and liaise with Sylvia on the Columba House stuff. She's chasing separate records. I don't want you falling over each other and giving them the impression that we're less than perfect. If that mob have anything to hide, I want it flushed out and I want them to know we're on to them.'

'Yes, sir.'

'Right, that's your starter for ten. Remember, we've got two dead kids to consider, tread very carefully. People are sensitive enough about the thought of a murder investigation. When kiddies are involved, sensitivity has a tendency to dip into hysteria.'

9

Night had crept in by the time DI Bob Valentine reached the door of the station. It had been a long day, longer than he had envisioned, and certainly one to remember. He could list the days on the job he had been genuinely shocked by events he was tasked to investigate; there had been a few – but none like today. As he had grown older, and grown into the role of detective inspector, the shocks had diminished, become fewer, to the point where it was almost impossible to be truly taken aback by anything.

When he thought about it dispassionately, Valentine wasn't moved by the crimes. He had ceased to be confounded by depravity or evil; he merely accepted they were part of life, like the rainfall or the changing of the tide. He could no more do anything about the fact that such things existed than he could stop the world turning. It would be futile to try.

That wasn't to say he welcomed their existence, or the feelings they engendered in him; he merely accepted evil-doing with a shrug. Part of him had changed along the way, hardened to the reality. It often felt like he'd grown an outer skin that was protecting him from the full impact. Perhaps there was a shield around his very human heart. It had been through so much, he wondered sometimes how it managed to keep going.

But amidst it all he knew that it wasn't in his interests to completely shut out the realities of the world, or totally protect his heart from their buffering. To do that was to diminish yourself, become less human, and then they had won. Valentine needed to remind himself from time to time that he was a man first and a cop second. He had a wife and children; he was the head of a family, not just a murder squad. If at any point one encroached on the other, he knew he was lost. But it was a hard fight and sometimes his vigilance slipped.

He got into the Vectra, started the engine and flicked on the lights. As he drove for home the night's darkness was spreading over the auld town. He saw the moonlight's silvery-white sheen reflected in the calmness of the River Ayr. The Town Hall's gargoyles, backlit with a greenish haze, added an air of the gothic to the scene. It seemed an unnatural place, Ayr's ancient cobbled streets and humpbacked bridges looking backwards to another time entirely.

Valentine rolled down the driver's window and tried to incur some of the breeze, in an attempt at cooling his head down. The persistent ache in his skull had settled into a cycle of dull lassitude and arresting misery, and he felt the latter approaching once more. He thought he knew what it meant, what it indicated to him, but he was still some way from fully accepting the explanation.

He distracted himself with how he might approach the impending conflict with his wife. Clare had every right to be upset with him coming home in the hours of darkness, missing yet another family meal and failing to spend any time with their teenage daughters.

His tendency was to avoid all conflict with Clare; he simply couldn't muster the energy or enthusiasm for argument any longer. And besides, he faulted himself for the failings of their marriage, not her. Clare was just trying to lead a normal life, but how could she do that when her husband was a man who disinterred the corpses of children for a living.

Valentine didn't know what he had become, what kind of man he was any more. All he knew was how to balance the vagaries of his chaotic and complicated existence; he knew how to find the balance, in principle, but in practice he also knew he often failed. Clare and the girls were the ones who suffered when that happened, and his worst fear was that they suffered more than him.

As he pulled in to his driveway in Masonhill, he spotted that a light was burning in the extension where they had homed his father. Valentine knew his dad was too frail to live alone, to look after himself, but as the memory of the church visit earlier in the day came back he wondered if his father really was better living under his son's roof. It seemed to Valentine that he had an uncanny knack of offloading his woes on those closest to him.

Closing the front door and laying down his briefcase, the DI loosened off his tie and looped it over the banister. There was no sign of Clare in the living room or the kitchen. She had left a plate of pasta, a side salad and a loaf of garlic bread beneath cling film for him. The thought of food at this late hour made him baulk; it was simply too much effort, but coffee seemed a worthwhile indulgence.

Valentine was filling the kettle when his father appeared from the door to the extension. At first he thought the old man was going to ignore him, but then he nodded sagely and the DI chided himself for thinking his dad would be so childish.

'I'm really sorry about today, Dad,' he said.

His father didn't reply, simply came over to stand beside his son, leaning on the counter and staring into the middle distance.

'It was a shock,' he said, 'to see you at Sandy's funeral like that.'

'I'm sure it must have been.'

'He was a good man, Sandy. A kindly soul. He didn't deserve to be treated like that.'

Valentine felt a long day getting longer; he didn't want to extend the misery. He didn't want to upset anyone, Sandy or his father, but he was doing his job. He had a sorely felt need to defend himself and his actions in the churchyard, but he resisted.

'I meant no offence to your friend, Dad. Or you, or Mam for that matter.'

His father turned his gaze on his son. 'I was very harsh with my words. I'm sorry.'

The kettle came to the boil. 'Would you like a coffee, Dad?'

The old man nodded.

The pair retreated to the living room and sat with their cups, facing each other but staring in different directions.

The old man spoke first. 'I suppose you must have had your reasons for what you did today.'

'Oh, you better believe it.' The words had come out

before he'd given them proper thought. 'What I mean is, it's a murder investigation.'

'In Cumnock?' He had his father's full attention.

'Ardinsh Farm.'

'Sandy's place?'

'It's not any more.'

'I don't understand.'

Valentine sipped at his coffee then started to rub the back of his neck. 'I'm not sure I do either.'

His father eased back in the armchair. 'I don't mean to pry.'

'It's not that, Dad. It's very complicated.'

'Can I be of any help?'

Valentine put down his cup. The taste of the coffee wasn't helping; it made him feel slightly nauseous. He detailed the day's events, drawing out the deaths as precisely as he could. He spoke about the boys in the barrel, how he had no idea who they were and how horrified he had been at the sight. Sandy Thompson, his farm and Garry Keirns he left until last. When he was sure he had covered everything, touched on his fears and quandaries, he sat back and observed his father's reaction.

The old man had listened in silence, and for a moment Valentine wondered if that was going to be his only reaction.

'I don't know what to say to that,' he said.

'Perhaps that's for the best. I must admit, a natural reaction is entirely beyond my experience too.'

'I feel terribly guilty for how I reacted at the church today. You must have been under the most enormous stress. Nobody should have to see a thing like that.'

'Dad, it's what I do.'

He shook his head. 'No, there's doing your duty and there's . . . that was something else. What you witnessed was inhumane. I can't imagine the impact it must have had on you, and then to have to rationalise it and make sense of what had to be done next. I don't know that I could function like that.'

'You get used to it.'

'I would never want to.'

'No. No one would.'

There was a long period where they sat in silence, his father sipping from the coffee cup in his hand. 'I thought we had it bad down the mines, I just – I never really thought of what you go through properly.'

Valentine tried to change the subject. 'So can you offer anything, perhaps about Sandy or the farm.'

The old man's expression changed. 'Now you're asking. You know he lost interest after Ida died.'

'Keirns said he was winding things down before he came on board.'

'That would be right. He fell into drink soon after.'

'I'd heard the rumours.'

'Yes, he was in a very bad way. I must confess I wasn't as good a friend as I should have been to him then; I stayed away.'

'I can't blame you.'

'It wasn't that – there was talk of drugs.'

'At Sandy's place?'

'No more than gossip. I've only got the word of loose mouths. They said he'd been taking drugs. You know the boy Garry had been involved in that sort of thing?'

'Just what is on his charge sheet. We're at the early stages of the investigation.'

61

'Garry came from the big house, the reformatory or whatever they call it. I suppose he'd learnt some bad habits there. There was talk he got Sandy on the drugs as well as the drink. He was always ferrying bottles back and forth to the farm, I know that – the taxi lads were forever saying. They'd keep a tally. It was bottles of whisky every day. I suppose he must have run through his savings pretty sharpish.'

'Did you know Sandy left Keirns the farm?'

He tutted. 'I'd heard as much.'

'You don't approve?'

'Why would I? What did he do to deserve it? He ran the bloody place into the ground.'

'He said it was Sandy's wishes.'

'And you believe that? Sandy wasn't sober a day past Ida's death. The poor bugger wouldn't know what he was signing away. Och, I'm off to bed. I'm getting myself all worked up again, and I'm not supposed to with my blood pressure.'

'Thanks, Dad.' He dropped his tone. 'Before you go, I saw Gerald Fallon at the funeral.'

'The MP?'

'Yes. Did Sandy know him?'

'Not to my knowledge. I must have missed Fallon myself.'

'He seemed to be leaving early.'

'Creeping out, more like. You know what the locals think of politicians after Thatcher.'

Valentine nodded. 'I thought it was a bit strange.'

'The world's all gone a bit strange, if you ask me. I'll say goodnight to you.'

'Goodnight, Dad.'

10

The house phone always seemed to ring louder first thing in the morning. Perhaps it was its situation next to his ear on the bedside table or the fact that it so seldom rang at all these days. He was more used to hearing his mobile, but it was definitely the landline blaring Valentine awake. He didn't know how long it had been ringing; it didn't seem that long a time, certainly not long enough for Clare to reach over him and pick up the receiver.

'Hello,' she said.

'Oh, hello, Mrs Valentine. I'm looking for the detective inspector.'

She threw the phone on top of the bedclothes. 'It's your little friend.'

'What?' He was still groggy from sleep and not fully awake yet, not quite removed from his dreams; not sure what was dream and what was reality.

'The one you spent the night with on Arran.' Clare's tone was acerbic and acted on the detective like smelling salts wafting beneath his nose.

Valentine promptly rose in the bed, covering the mouthpiece. 'Why did you say that?'

'Well you did spend the night with her.'

'I did not . . . we did *not* spend the night together.'

'Yes you did.' Clare was getting out of bed, slipping her arms into her dressing gown and drawing the cord tightly round her waist. 'You told me yourself about the cosy tryst at the Auchrannie.'

Valentine couldn't believe what he was hearing. 'It was work. The last ferry had left.'

'How convenient.' His wife mocked him with a smirk and headed through the bedroom door.

As he watched the door closing Valentine wondered what had prompted the outburst. He knew there didn't need to be a direct reason – Clare was good at storing things up – but it didn't bode well. As he removed his hand from the mouthpiece and raised the phone to his ear, he noticed the blue folder he had brought to bed for late-night reading sitting beside him on the table and sighed, involuntarily, into the phone.

'Yes . . .'

'Not a good time, sir?' said DS McCormack.

'Is there such a thing?'

She didn't reply. 'We have a slot with the pathologist at 8.30, is that doable?'

'What time is it now?'

'It's 7.15.'

'Yes, I suppose we can always turn up in the middle of things if we don't beat the traffic.'

'Would you like me to pick you up, boss?'

'I suppose there's no point taking two cars.'

'OK, I'll be at your front door in half an hour.'

'Eh, no.' Valentine thought better of the arrangement. 'Pick me up at the station. I'll leave my car there. It'll save me coming out here to get it if I need it later.'

'Whatever you say.'

He changed the topic. 'Is there any news this morning, Sylvia?'

'News, sir?'

'On the case?'

'We have the site listing from the SOCOs. It's very lengthy but also a bit short on detail.'

'There's probably a fuller one with pictures on the way. Bring it anyway; I'll give it the once-over in the car. Anything else?'

'Not really, too early for calls to be returned yet. Oh, I think Ally spent the night in the basement. No one has seen hide nor hair of him since about midnight when he visited the coffee machine and popped in.'

'Let's hope he's found something worthwhile, as opposed to a lot of nonsense that will drive us to distraction for weeks to come.'

'Let's. I'll see you later, boss.'

'Oh, before you go, give Davie Purves a call and set up a meeting somewhere that suits him. Probably won't be Cumnock because he's one of those ex-cops that don't like being seen talking to cops.'

'I was going to do that anyway. Are you saying you want to be there too?'

'I think so, might be better to afford him some rank. And I might get further playing the old pals act with him.'

'OK. Incidentally, whilst we're on the subject of meeting people, I spoke to Crosbie last night. He's happy to have a chat with you too.'

'Bloody hell, Sylvia.'

'I thought you said . . .'

'Yes, look, you're probably right. I should speak to him, especially after the night I had.'

Valentine showered and dressed. He knew he had left his shoes downstairs so he could creep into bed without waking Clare but he questioned the logic now. If she was going to be upset about another murder investigation that took him from home, he might have been better facing it promptly and getting it out of the way. Leaving things to fester was never a good idea.

When he got downstairs and walked into the kitchen Clare was sitting at the breakfast bar with a cigarette burning in front of her. She'd made coffee and indicated the pot to him.

'Thank you, I'd love a cup,' said Valentine.

Clare poured out the coffee and said the milk was in the fridge. 'I must have sounded like a right harpy this morning.'

He was relieved her mood had changed. 'It's all right. I shouldn't have brought this up.' Valentine tapped on the blue folder under his arm then laid it down on the counter as he poured milk into his coffee.

'I'm sick of you doing this job, Bob.'

'You've made your feelings felt on the issue.'

She picked up her cigarette and inhaled. 'It can be fine for a time, weeks even. I didn't mind you working that missing-persons thing, or the burglaries, but my mind works overtime when I see the murder squad coming home with you.'

'Clare . . .'

'No, let me finish. You don't seem to get it, no matter what I say. It's not about me – it's about you. You nearly

66

died. You *did* die for Christ's sake, and you're not the same man.'

'I'm fine now – that was some time ago.'

'It wasn't. We nearly lost you for good, Bob. The girls nearly lost a father. How do you think that would be for them growing up without a dad – or for me?'

'I thought it wasn't about you?' It was a silly thing to say, petty, and Valentine regretted it immediately. 'I'm sorry.'

'You see, you're on edge already. Think of the stress that puts on your heart, never mind the stress it puts on us.'

Valentine stirred his coffee; the first sip revived his spirits slightly. 'We've been here before. It's my job. We have commitments – the remortgaging for the extension, Fiona's going to be off to uni soon – how will we pay for it all?' He made a conscious effort not to mention Clare's credit-card debts; her shopping addiction had cost them enough already.

'There's other jobs, Bob.'

'I don't know anything else.'

'I could get a job.' The idea was almost laughable to Valentine. His wife had never worked a day in her life. She had been a proud mother and homemaker, and she'd excelled at both. She had no idea what the world of work took from you.

'Clare, I don't want to see you sitting behind a till at bloody Asda.'

'Is that all you think I'm worth?'

'No. I mean, be realistic, you're not qualified . . . why are we even having this conversation? We have it every time I lead a murder investigation.'

Clare stood up and tightened her dressing gown around

her waist. The cigarette before her had almost burnt itself out, a long cylinder of grey ash curling down into the tray. She reached over and stubbed it out.

'OK then, no more. I won't say another word. But you can deal with the consequences.'

Valentine put his hand on hers. 'What's that supposed to mean, love?'

She jerked her hand away. 'It means what it means.'

'Clare, come on, would you listen to yourself?'

'No, Bob, you listen to me. I want you to ask for a new job, a transfer back to the training college, something away from the front line.'

'I can't do that. The force is stretched to breaking point; they need all the experienced manpower they can get.'

'I mean it. Ask for a move, or it'll be me who's moving on, and I'm not kidding this time.'

The door from the extension opened and Valentine's father stepped through. 'Oh, hello, lovely morning.'

He was met with frosty silence and averted gazes.

'Was it something I said?' There was no reply from Valentine or Clare. 'I think I'll go back out and come in again.'

'No, Dad, come away in. I'm just leaving anyway.' The DI couldn't bring himself to make eye contact with his wife as he went.

11

The early-morning drive to Glasgow passed without traffic disruption, except for the usual snare up on the Kingston Bridge. The sun appeared to favour the city over Ayr today, even managing to push the morning rays through a canopy of cloud covering the sky. Valentine observed DS McCormack's mood brightening too, as it always did when she returned home. She tapped a beat with her fingertips on the gearstick as she drove towards the morgue; it was only mildly disconcerting to the DI to have such a chipper travel partner so early in the morning.

'How are you getting on with the list, sir?' said McCormack.

The DI looked up from the pages. 'There's some interesting details, if it is a little sketchy.'

'We should have the bagged-up artefacts in the incident room later today; the photogs are still working on them. I thought what we do have already paints an interesting picture of the two boys.'

Valentine put down the report. 'They're clearly from very different backgrounds.'

'Do you think they knew each other? I mean, how would you know that? But it seems likely.'

'I'm not assuming anything at this stage, Sylvia. Except that one of the boys was fairly well-to-do and one not so much.'

McCormack indicated to change lanes; they were entering the city centre and slowing with the increasing traffic. 'Did you see the rosary, sir?'

'Yeah, and a St Christopher pendant – but no chain. It doesn't say if there's anything engraved on the back. It could belong to a St John's pupil, which is the Catholic school, but the listing for the school tie doesn't say what it looks like.'

'What did they look like?'

'St John's ties were striped – blue, black and white.'

'I'll check that when we get parked, sir. It's just a phone call. That would be the better-off boy, I take it?'

'Yeah.' Valentine's gaze wandered over the cityscape. 'I think I remember a boy going missing from there, a while back now. Was I still at school myself? Can't quite recall the details, if he was found or not.'

'What about the other boy, anything standing out?'

'Everything seems so well preserved. There's school jotters and a comic, football stickers but no bloody details! There could be names sewn into their clothes and we don't know going by this list.' Valentine returned to the report. 'The other kid, yeah, elbow patches on the grey V-neck, a penknife and a bookie's pen in the pocket of the shorts, and tackity boots – contrast those to the Clarks' shoes on the other lad. They were definitely from opposite sides of the tracks.'

As they pulled up outside the morgue McCormack yanked on the handbrake. 'You go in, sir. I'll call the photogs and see if they can shed some light on this.'

'All right. But hurry up, I want you to see Wrighty's work.'

Valentine headed for the pathology department and made his way to the morgue. Once briskly dressed for the procedure he approached Wrighty, who was talking into a microphone that dangled over the slab. Both the boys' bodies were laid out, side by side; they seemed smaller and more shrivelled than the DI ever imagined.

'They look so tiny,' he said.

The pathologist steadied the mic to stop it swinging. 'Another human tragedy with horrific consequences.'

Valentine made a closer inspection of the corpse he had seen the previous day. He was surprised that it didn't smell a lot worse. 'The smell's gone.'

'Mummified remains are virtually odourless. The soil might have been damp – that's probably what you were smelling.'

'So you have experience of this sort of thing then?'

'Oh, yes. Surprisingly common, though normally it's mummified bairns I see. When they die young and get shoved in a drawer or the back of an airing cupboard it's the perfect conditions to ward off putrefaction. That's all it is by the way, a denial of the usual order of decay.'

Valentine eyed the second corpse. The head was pressed into the shoulder at an unnatural angle. The black, leathery, skeletal features of the face looked very peaceful by contrast.

'Can you tell me what went on here, Wrighty?'

The pathologist took a deep breath, like he was about to stick his head underwater. 'I don't know about that, but I can hazard a guess as to cause of death in both cases.'

'Go on then.'

He moved towards the DI. 'Let's start with this lad. Incidentally, I don't know if it's any use to you, but when we undressed him we found his Y-fronts had been put on back to front. I thought that was unusual.'

Valentine looked at the shrunken figure; he noticed the dissection line down his chest and stomach, the crooked detour taken by the scalpel around the belly button. 'It might be something, it might not.'

'Well, they've both got the same PMI, I can confirm that.'

'Speak English please.'

'The post-mortem interval – the time of death – is about thirty-two years ago, so that takes us down to 1984.'

'The police surgeon was about seven years out then. What about their ages?'

'I was coming to that. This one is about eleven; the other one about a year younger.'

The door to the morgue opened and DS McCormack walked towards the men. 'Sorry, sir, the school tie's too soiled to make out. They're going to sample test a section . . . Hello, Wrighty.'

The pathologist nodded and returned to the slab in front of him. 'Look at the neck on the eleven-year-old – see how it's contorted? That's because something's bitten into the neck. You can see the flesh has been torn in the manner of a garrotte. I had him down as asphyxia due to strangulation, but I couldn't find the device used. Looks like a belt – a thick leather belt would cause deep cuts like that.'

'So you think he was strangled?'

'No, hold your horses, Bob, he was definitely strangled.'

Wrighty retrieved an X-ray slide from a table and held it to the light. 'Look, there's two broken cervical vertebrae – that seals it. He was strangled.'

Wrighty moved up the slab towards the other corpse. 'This one's hands and feet were cable-tied; he was restrained obviously.'

'Was he strangled too?' said Valentine.

'Oh no. This boy was bludgeoned to death. Let me show you the rear of the scalp; it's been split in two places, which made me think he'd been battered with something.'

'We've no murder weapon. What should we be looking for?'

'You're the cop, Bob. But it's been something blunt and heavy, a hammer maybe. If you look closer to the rear of the head there you'll see it was driven with sufficient force to shatter the skull. The X-ray confirmed that – there's fragments of bone separated from the occipital region. It would have been driven into the brain with the force from the blunt instrument and killed him instantly.'

Valentine watched Wrighty as he paused with his finger-tips on the rim of the mortuary slab.

'Is there anything else you can tell me?' said the DI.

'Isn't that enough?'

'You know me – always after more if I can get it.'

Wrighty shrugged. 'I can tell you this, it might have been thirty-two years ago, but I'd do time for the bastard that did this.'

They looked at the corpses of the two boys but nobody spoke again. Wrighty's last words seemed to sum up how everyone felt about the case. There was nothing to add, only the painful realisation of how two young boys had been brutally murdered. Even though the way they'd been found had indicated the worst, knowing the precise details of their demise somehow shared more of the pain around.

Valentine and McCormack headed back to the car, the DI offering to drive.

'Go for it, here's the keys,' said McCormack.

Valentine took the keys and reached for the door handle. 'Do you want to hear just the funniest thing, Sylvia? That headache I had has completely vanished now.'

12

June 1982

'Out,' shouts the man with a nose like a hawk.

It looks like we're at some kind of parade ground. I can see a small coach house made of bricks with black bars on the windows. There's a chimney pumping smoke out for all to see.

When I get to the steps of the bus I'm told to move myself and that I'm not here for the view. The bus driver laughs at that and says, 'Far from it.'

I don't know what he means, but I know it can't be good. The ground's brick too, or I think it is, till the man catches me looking at it and says get used to them cobbles and I'll be keeping a sheen on them with my boots.

I'm thinking about what's been said when I spot the big house. At the end of the parade there's black, iron bollards with chains linking them leading all the way to the stone steps. The house is bigger than any I've seen before; it's grey but not bricks this time. There's too many windows to count, hundreds really, and a big old door open out front.

Inside I see more doors, and beyond them a twisty hand-rail that wends its way up a giant staircase. The stairs are bare – no carpets, just white paint – and there's two boys on their knees with bristle brushes scrubbing away. One boy has a pail of water and they both dip into it, but they stop what they're doing to stare at the coach and me. When the man with a nose like a hawk appears he grabs my collar and the boys turn away.

'This way,' he says, and he birls me around and shoves me towards the smaller place with the bars on the window. In there he stands talking to another man, who sits down. There's some joking, and I think they've forgotten about me and maybe we're not here to stay, that maybe we're just waiting to go somewhere else, that maybe someone is coming to get me. I don't like the place, not one bit.

'You, boy,' he shouts at me. 'You, boy, get stripped.'

I don't know what he's saying. He gets up, still roaring, and points me to another door. It's a washroom. I see the other man, the one with a nose like a hawk, go out the door we just came in.

There's great orange tiles on the floor and walls and only a small window where the light gets in from outside, but it's up high and has bars outside in case I was planning an escape. The water comes on from above, and the shower head splutters at first, and then it breaks into great jets.

'Strip! Strip!' shouts the man who's off the seat now. He's baldy and carries a great round belly in front of him. He looks mad, angry. I don't know at what.

'Get the bloody clothes off, boy, and get that scabby face of yours washed before I have to look at you again.' He hands me a bar of soap. It's strange soap, yellow but almost transparent too. The soap smells of medicine.

76

'You'll feel the lash of my belt if I have to tell you again,' he bawls at me.

He doesn't have to tell me again.

I shower for maybe an hour. It seems longer. He says I can come out when the soap's gone but there's still a great ball of it. I think of eating it, but the smell is terrible and makes me feel sick.

When the showers stop, I stand there in the washroom, on the orange tiles, and start to shiver. I shiver for long enough. I expect a towel or something, but there's no towel. I look for my clothes, but they're gone.

After a while the bald man shows up with a wicker basket. There's a pewter bottle on top. He spins me round and pours something like talc on me, but it's not the talc I know. He lifts up my arms and throws it there and on my bits. It smells like the worst of shite. I'm glad when he leaves me, pointing at the basket and saying, 'Dress yourself.'

They're somebody else's clothes; they've been worn before. The shirt's too big; it's got stains on the front. It's kind of grey, but I think it might have been a different colour altogether once. The collars and cuffs are frayed. There's more shorts there too, black this time, and stiff as cardboard. I hate them. I have no shoes.

'Right, up the house.'

'What about shoes?'

'Up the house – there's shoes there.'

I go outside in my bare feet and follow the black bollards with the chains. I keep standing on little stones and when I yelp the bald man tells me to shut up or he'll give me something to yelp about.

'This way . . . No, through here . . . In there.'

We reach the kitchen. It's the biggest kitchen I've ever seen. There's a black range with a little door on the front where a woman puts coal. She's older than Mammy was. I wonder who she is and will she be nice, but she doesn't say a thing, only puts down a plate of yellow mush called swede and a piece of bread. The bread is too hard to bite, but I'm famished so I find a way.

The baldy man goes now; he tells me to wait for the master. I eat every scrap of food and lick the plate clean, and the woman says don't let the master see you doing that. She takes the plate as he appears in the door, tall and thin, a full suit of clothes and a shirt with a tie and a pin in it.

He says, 'Feet. C'mon, show me your feet.'

I bring my feet from under the table and he looks down at them, then he disappears back through the door. In a minute he's back, measuring a boot against my foot.

'Try it on.'

'It's too big,' I say.

'Well that's better than too small.'

He makes me walk up and down the kitchen and watches every step I take, his hands resting on his hips. I think of everyone I've seen so far he frightens me the most. He doesn't talk much, doesn't shout, but I think he doesn't need to because he's the master and he knows it.

I think of Mammy again, and the squat, and how it ended, but I still think I'd sooner be there. I want it all to have been a bad dream, so I can wake up and see Mammy and have my old clothes back and be how things used to be. But I know now that's not going to happen, and things are going to be very different, and I don't like any of it.

13

'I didn't know you could still find places like this,' said DS McCormack.

'They're there – you're just not looking hard enough,' said Valentine, unfastening his jacket buttons as they approached the bar.

The last time they'd visited there had been an old rockabilly behind the bar; Valentine remembered the swallow tattoo on the man's hand and the Brylcreemed hair. He had an eye for distinguishing features that he'd honed over the years.

Their server today was an elderly woman in a pink tabard. Her white hair was permed into corkscrews, a look that couldn't have changed for decades. She wore a dirty pair of tartan slippers behind the bar and had an NHS-issue walking stick leaning against the till. Valentine found her presence soothing in its familiarity, and the mood of the bar was relaxing in its complete lack of pretension.

'I do tend to shy away from working men's clubs,' said McCormack. 'Could be because I'm a woman and not a relic of the days of yore.'

'It's probably that you're from Glasgow. There's precious little industry left on either bank of the Clyde.'

'What's the phrase? You can credit Thatcher for bringing salmon back to the River Clyde.'

Valentine smiled. 'That's the first positive thing I've ever heard credited to that woman.'

'Careful, your Cumnock's showing.'

The DI ordered two Cokes. They came in cans accompanied by empty glasses.

'Can I have some ice please?' said McCormack.

The old woman rolled her eyes as she returned to the bar to retrieve an ice bucket. Valentine and McCormack smiled together, the DS muttering, 'I'm so extravagant.'

They chose a table at the front of the pub, beside a window with yellowing net curtains. Valentine picked up a beer mat and started sweeping stray crisp crumbs on to the floor. 'Why did you pick this place, Sylvia?'

'I didn't. It's Crosbie's local.' She looked at her watch. 'He should be here in ten minutes.'

Valentine's gaze wandered around the tired room. 'I can hardly believe you've got me into this again. We have a murder investigation underway you know.'

'Sir, I think this is important. And he did help you the last time.'

Valentine mockingly glanced over his shoulder, pretending to shiver. 'I wonder what spirits surround me today?'

The DS started to pour her drink into the glass, the black liquid fizzing over the ice. 'You said something about having a bad night . . .'

'I've had worse.'

'Was it like before, on the other cases?'

'It's hard to tell; it was very confused. Images mainly.

That's what Crosbie said last time, that I needed to learn to interpret their messages.'

'Whose messages? The people in the dreams?'

'I didn't ask.'

'I told him about your stomach pains and the sore head. He said that's very common.'

'Did he?' Valentine was surprised – the pain felt very particular to him. He couldn't imagine an outbreak occurring any time soon.

'He said the pains were a response to your questioning mind – you got the answers you asked for.'

Valentine stared at his drink. It seemed a better option than directing his attention to the DS. 'I suppose that makes a sort of sense. On both occasions, the stomach and the head pains, I was looking for the cause of death.'

'And on both occasions the answer was uncannily accurate.'

Valentine didn't reply. It wasn't that he didn't agree with McCormack, he just felt that any such conversation should be held with a dose of mockery thrown in.

The conversation waned. Both officers checked their watches again. An awkward silence started to stretch out.

'Look, tell me if I'm being out of order, boss, but I heard what your wife said to you this morning.'

Valentine looked up. 'On the phone?'

'The bit about Arran, about us spending the night together.'

'You heard that, did you?'

McCormack nodded.

'I'm sorry about that. Clare has a strange way of expressing herself sometimes.'

'She sounded serious enough.'

'Well, she wasn't, trust me. If she believed that she'd already have gone.'

'Already?'

Valentine slumped back in his chair, his shoulders deflated. 'She wants me to ask for a transfer, off the murder squad. Says she's leaving me this time if I don't.'

McCormack flustered. Her eyelids seemed to close for longer than they should as she composed herself. 'I don't know what to say. I'm sorry.'

'Why? It's nothing to do with you.'

'But if she thinks we slept together . . .'

'Sylvia, that's just her bad streak. No, wait, I don't mean that. Clare has the biggest heart I know, she's a very sensitive woman, and when she feels threatened she sometimes overreacts, do you understand?'

'I know people like her.'

'She knows what I've been going through, but she knows nothing about it – the subject, I mean – so she's envious that you can help me, that's all. And she's weak and hard on herself and sees threats where there are none.'

'I understand. She means everything to you, doesn't she?'

'My family is my life, Sylvia.'

'I can't imagine ever understanding someone like you've just spoken of Clare.'

'I sometimes wonder if I even understand myself half as well. Especially since the stabbing and all this head stuff started.'

As Crosbie appeared at the door he waved and approached their table. His walk was brisk, businesslike.

He had the air of an accountant or another professional. It was reassuring to Valentine, who still couldn't quite decide if the man was a kook or not. The officers rose. Valentine and Crosbie exchanged handshakes.

'Can I get you a drink?' said McCormack.

'A soft drink would be fine,' said Crosbie.

He settled into the vacant chair as McCormack made for the bar. He didn't bother with small talk, instead addressing Valentine's problem directly.

'Sylvia tells me you are experiencing some level of distress.'

'I suppose that's one way of putting it.'

Crosbie removed his scarf and jacket, placing them over the back of his chair. His black lambswool jumper made him look like clergy to Valentine, who tried to suppress the image as Crosbie spoke again. 'Everyone goes through this shock when they discover these abilities. I felt like I was walking on the moon when I realised I could use the sight.'

'The sight?'

'I always found that a strange term myself, especially as it's more of a feeling. Perhaps insight would be better.'

Valentine watched McCormack put down Crosbie's drink. He thanked her. 'Sylvia says you had pains relating to your victims' passing. I want to assure you that's very common. There's nothing to fear at all – it's just a means of communication.'

'Isn't that just your interpretation?' said Valentine. 'I mean couldn't it just be a coincidence?'

'No. Not to me. But you can think that if you like. I don't know how far you'd get blocking them out, mind you.'

The DI felt he had ruffled Crosbie. 'I don't mean to sound disrespectful.'

'You don't. You sound sceptical, just as you did when we last spoke. I told you then not to try and rationalise any of this or understand it with the tools you use in the everyday world.'

'I just find that very difficult. It goes against the grain for me.'

'Because you're a rational man, Bob. You use reason and deduction daily, you use your mind to rationalise what you don't understand, but this . . . these discoveries you are experiencing can't be understood that way – they won't subject themselves to the rational mind.'

'That's what I have a problem with.'

'OK. Then let me ask you this. How do you read? How do you write? Spell? Add up?'

'You just do, just the way you were taught.'

'You missed the question. I didn't ask how it was done, but how you do it, how your mind does it? No one can answer that – it's a mystery. The mind is the greatest mystery of them all; no one can understand or explain how it works, but you seem to demand just that. Your belief isn't tied to understanding, it exists in and of itself, whether you accept it or not.'

Valentine was silenced. He understood perfectly what Crosbie was telling him, but it made little difference to what he was experiencing. He raised his glass, hoping to hide the contemplation on his face.

McCormack spoke. 'I think Bob's a bit shell shocked by it all.'

'Of course,' said Crosbie. 'And you're not the first either, Bob. I was just as sceptical as you.'

'Then how did you reach this level of understanding?' said Valentine.

'I accepted nothing, but I trusted myself. So I tested myself. I asked questions of these abilities, and I got answers. I suppose I became a little obsessed then. I asked lots of questions – looked at lots of answers too. I didn't realise it, but I was training my sight, this insight, and soon I realised that it was so effective that I couldn't question it. That's when I found acceptance, and you will too, Bob, when you stop doubting yourself.'

Valentine reached for his drink and drew a large draught. He felt the pressure of contradiction all around him. He found he could agree and disagree with Crosbie at the same time. If he played with these thoughts enough, he knew, he would reach only mental exhaustion. But he would have to concede to one strain of thought at some point.

'And how do you test yourself?' said the DI.

'How do you test anything? Set a challenge. Don't wait for it to come to you, don't wait for spirits to channel through you, call on them.'

'Now, hang on, that sounds just . . .'

'Be open-minded, Bob. Not with what I'm saying. Don't get hung up on the words. Remember none of this can be understood at the level of words. Just give way to it and see what happens.'

'You mean ask for answers to specific questions?'

'You did before. You said yourself you were asking for the cause of death and your victim told you. The answers came to you because the energy was drawn to you. You can seek energy out like that.'

'But how? I mean, at a simple level, do I just ask fresh air for answers?'

Crosbie clasped his hands together. His voice came low and deep. 'You'll find what works for you. I tend to go into deep relaxation; others put themselves in a trance state. You can even have an assistant help count you down or talk you through it. Of course sometimes the energy comes from other sources. Possessions hold the imprints of their owner's souls. These images can point to you. In time you'll be able to manipulate the images, even see through the eyes of those that have passed.'

'It sounds incredible.'

'It is, Bob. Life is incredible. But so is death. Can you honestly say you understand more than a very little about either?'

14

At King Street station Valentine checked in with Jim Prentice on the front desk. Prentice was crouched over some paper-work behind the countertop, a tightly held fist pressing into his forehead. As Valentine appeared, Prentice looked up but just as quickly returned his attention to the papers.

'Just a minute, Bob,' he said. 'Bloody rota juggling again.'

'I take it that it's a staff shortage, not the other way around.'

He put down his pen and shoved away the rotas. 'No, actually. There's too many on now according to Dino. She wants numbers at the operational minimal to save on wages.'

'It's a false economy.'

'It's no bloody economy at all. It means the desk goes unmanned between two and three-thirty. Either that or muggins here has to sit with a sandwich in his lap whilst Stellard and Brandt shoot off to the canteen.'

The DI gave a consoling shake of the head. 'She better not get any ideas about short-changing my murder inves-tigation. That isn't happening.'

Prentice lit up. 'Oh, aye, the mummy – how's that play-ing out?'

'Everything's a mystery.'

'I hear they've got two now.'

'Two boys, ten and eleven.'

'Horrible business. Just a tragic case. I can hardly bring myself to think about it.'

'We're talking thirty-two years ago as well. It would be even more tragic if the trail runs cold.'

'Let me know if there's anything I can do,' said Prentice. 'But not between two and three-thirty!'

The DI thanked the desk sergeant and collected a Post-it note detailing messages that had been passed through to the incident room.

'I think they're for you, Sylvia.' He handed over the note.

'Ah, yes. Looks like Keirns's social-security records and a return number for Columba House.'

'Nothing from Blairgowan?'

'Unless it went straight upstairs, boss. I've nothing here or on my phone.'

'Did you ask them specifically about the offer on the farm?'

'Yes. I didn't mention Keirns to them though. Thought it was better to let them volunteer the information.'

Valentine moved for the stairs and the DS followed. By the time he reached the landing outside the incident room the DI had reassessed the situation. 'If they haven't called, call again – and don't take any bullshit.'

'I was going softly, sir. Phil said they weren't the most helpful at the site. Seemed a bit of a cowboy outfit, albeit one that had moved on from being a white-van crew.'

'I heard him. We'll see how helpful they get when I go up there and shut the site down for them today.'

'Is that your plan, sir?'

Valentine pushed open the swing doors to the incident room and went through. The hum of activity stalled for a second or two then resumed its previous pace.

'Put it this way, Sylvia, if Blairgowan don't play straight with us then we won't be playing straight with them either.'

'Yes, boss.'

The DI's thoughts had already shifted to another aspect of the case – there was so much to think about in the early stages of a murder investigation. He summoned DS Donnelly to him.

'Phil, a minute please.'

'Yes, sir.'

'What have I missed whilst we were away?'

Donnelly rubbed his jaw. 'Well, Wrighty's sent through the preliminary post-mortem report, but I suppose you'll know more about what he uncovered than the rest of us.'

The officers had settled at DS McCormack's desk. When she had hung up her coat and stuffed her bag beneath the desk she started to remove her chair. 'There's some details still to be coloured in by the SOCOs,' she said.

'The catalogue's in – well, the full photographer's listings,' said Phil.

'Great. We'll start there. Let's see them,' said Valentine.

DS Donnelly moved to the other end of the room and retrieved some folders from a set of stacking trays beneath the whiteboard. As he walked back he continued addressing the two officers who had just come in. 'I haven't been through all of these or stuck any up on the board. It's been a bit mad in here, and I seem to be flying solo.'

'Where's Ally?' said Valentine. DS McCormack was on the telephone now. She shrugged by way of response.

'He's in the bloody basement. I can't get him out of there.'

'He's been in there since last night.'

'I think he might have found some of Rossi's old *Razzle* mags.'

'Christ, if that's the case we'll never see him again. Or him us for that matter.'

The officers laughed at the absent DS McAlister.

'If he's not back soon, send in a search party, Phil.'

'Will do, sir.' DS Donnelly laid down the folders and they started to go through the photographs. Valentine was first to alight upon a picture of one of the boys' footwear.

'Heavy duty, eh?' said Donnelly.

'They look army issue, if the forces were hard up enough to use segs.'

'Segs?'

'You've never heard of segs? I suppose they're well before your time.' Valentine pointed to the kidney-shaped metal fixings on the heels of the boots. 'There, you hammered them in like nails to make the soles last longer.'

'Looks medieval, boss.'

'You're obviously not a miner's son – certainly not one that sat on the lines during the strike.'

'You're telling me you had these in your boots as a nipper, boss?'

Valentine smirked. 'Only my Sunday ones.'

'I think my leg's being pulled.'

'Maybe just a little, but you wouldn't believe me if I told you about the handmade clogs.'

Donnelly laughed. 'Now you are kidding.'

'All joking aside, these pictures tell an interesting story, don't you think?'

The DS watched Valentine sifting through the photographs. 'I went through the evidence bags this morning and took some notes, sir.'

'Do we have the tie back from forensic?'

'Not yet. But I think we can pretty much narrow that down to the Catholic school.'

'St John's.'

'That's it. We have a rosary and a St Christopher too. I can't see those being any use to a lad from the other school.'

'That's for sure.'

'The St Christopher had an engraving on the back, nothing too informative, just the initials C. B. S.'

Valentine thought about the information the DS had just provided. 'It might help us ID him down the track. Maybe someone will recognise it.'

'It's the kind of thing a mother would give him, if he was maybe going away or travelling. I know my mam gave me one about that age to take to Blackpool on a school trip.'

As Valentine listened to Donnelly he could hear his voice softening. The emotion was breaking in; it was going to be one of those cases. 'It's not for me to tell you how to process this stuff, Phil, but try not to become too attached.'

'I know, I know, sir.' He nodded. 'It's just that they were only kiddies.'

McCormack slammed down the telephone's receiver and cursed loudly behind the detectives, breaking their reverie completely.

'Bloody waste of space!' she said.

'Blairgowan?' said Valentine.

'You heard me asking for Freddie Gowan – he's the top man.'

'And?'

'And Mr Gowan has a woman who keeps his diary, and she isn't in the office today – she's with him on site.'

'Our site?' said Valentine.

'Unless they've another one in Cumnock.'

'Well, I'll save you waiting for a callback that might be too late in coming for my liking.'

'Sir?'

'Get your coat. You too, Phil. We're going to pay Mr Gowan a visit. And he's about to find out that a police murder scene trumps a building site by a country mile.'

15

The SOCOs seemed to be gathering soil samples when the detectives arrived. The uniform presence had diminished to two officers hovering around the doors of the white tent and a further one inside a police Land Rover. It was an old Discovery, the wheel arches and tyres splashed with more mud than it looked used to, but Valentine doubted it had been pressed into action as a 4x4 on this occasion.

The track he had taken through the field was still evident, the grass yellowing slightly in the hazy, yet very welcome, July sunshine. Rain had been the more natural course followed by the Ayrshire weather over the last few days, but the detective would settle for blue skies and birdsong whenever it was on offer.

'Brightening up,' said Valentine.

'Careful, you'll jinx it and have us calling in for wellies,' said McCormack.

They proceeded to the tent and peered through the open door. It was lighter inside than on the last visit, the brighter skies and sunshine helping, but much of what passed for official business had already been undertaken.

'Hello there, Bob.' A small, white mask was pulled down to reveal a greying goatee beard and a prominent smile.

'Bernie, how's the clean-up going?'

'We've got pretty much the lot, just taking some soil readings but they won't be over analysed. It's clear the scene of crime hasn't moved in the thirty-odd years we're looking at now.'

'You mean the oil drum's been in the ground the whole time?'

'That's what the oxidation would suggest. The pH levels on the soil are consistent, and there's no sign of foreign bodies or secondary intrusion. It'd be my guess the boys have rested here, if not in peace, certainly undisturbed for the whole time.'

'We're getting the barrel looked at too,' said Valentine. 'In case it can tell us anything.'

The scenes of crime officer started to mop his brow and headed for the door. 'Probably wise, if a long shot. Let's grab some air, eh.'

'Sure.'

'I wouldn't hold out too many hopes on the oil drum. It's ICI – you realise that's like trying to pin down a can of Pepsi!'

'Really, that common?'

'From that period, yes. They were utilised a lot agriculturally as well. I grew up on a farm, and I can remember them coming and going all the time. We used them for rafting and on the floats at the local parade – it was probably just what came to hand on this occasion too.'

'It certainly fitted its use. Almost tailor-made for those two wee boys.'

The conversation trailed off, neither man appearing inclined to continue with the topic. There was nothing that could be said that would help the situation – or the boys. 'How long are you planning to camp out here, Bernie?'

'We're just about done.'

Valentine looked around the crime scene; the path he'd come stretched through a field all the way to a drystone dyke at the road. To the west was the farmhouse, looking depressed and abandoned, its windows shuttered and the front door crudely planked over. Eastwards lay the heavily scarred tracks of the excavator, a stationary JCB digger and a partially laid road cavity. Further to the east were a number of concrete pipeworks, manhole coverings and a neatly stacked row of culvert drainage beds. The group of men in high-visibility overalls and hard hats seemed motionless, merely watching the goings of the officers at the farmyard.

'I'm going to have to ask you to hang fire, Bernie,' said the DI.

'Why's that?'

Valentine pointed towards the decrepit farmhouse. 'I want your team to give the interior of that place the once-over. I say once-over, what I really mean is I want everything pulled up and looked at, including the floorboards.'

'Fair enough. Better hearing this now I suppose than when we're all off site. Can I ask what you're looking for in particular?'

'Whatever you can pick up. One of the boys was bludgeoned, so a murder weapon of the blunt-instrument variety would be an enormous help. The other was strangled. Anything that could be used as a ligature would likewise be a good find.'

The SOCO looked doubtful. 'You're the boss, Bob.'

'I know that thirty-two years down the track it's a bloody long shot, but I'm not in a position to disregard the long odds on this one.'

'I understand. But do you understand that thirty-two years is a long time for site contamination to build up? The chances of us finding anything are slim, and the chances of a court admitting any random finds are precisely nil.'

'Those two boys were killed somewhere. If it was in there, maybe we'll find a trace of it. If it's an inadmissible trace so be it. Maybe it will point us to something that's more helpful.'

Valentine made for the excavator tracks and the gathering of workers; the beginnings of the new road had halted almost directly between the farmhouse and the bourne of the Columba House estate. Neither building looked thankful for the intrusion.

'Who's the gaffer?' said Valentine. The workers seemed to be preoccupied with their boots and the *Daily Mirror*; no one answered.

'Like that, is it?' said the DI.

A man in a denim shirt stepped away from the group. 'We've been warned not to talk to the cops, mate.'

'That right?'

He shrugged. An inverted grin appeared in the middle of his heavy, red beard. 'Sorry. If you go down to the foot of the brae you'll maybe have better luck.'

Valentine nodded in the direction the man indicated. 'Towards the Jag?'

'Aye. That's the man you want.'

'Is that Gowan?'

'You'll get Freddie Gowan and the site manager down

there, maybe even catch the foreman if he's not been sent out for the tea.'

Valentine thanked the worker and proceeded down the easy slope of the hill towards the burgundy Jaguar. As he got closer, two men came into focus. They were leaning over the bonnet of the car, examining what looked like a site map.

'Mr Gowan?'

'Yes, Freddie Gowan.' He was heavyset with a broad face and a black moustache. His dark eyes took in Valentine with an upward and downward glance that suggested he either didn't rate the detective's appearance or was irked by the intrusion.

'DI Valentine.' He presented his warrant card. 'I believe someone from my squad has been in touch with you.'

'I don't answer the phones.'

Valentine put away his wallet. 'I'm sure you don't. But now that I have you here, perhaps you could answer some questions for me.'

Gowan shrugged. He pointed to the map on the car and his colleague started to fold it away. 'I'll try.'

'This investment, has it been on the cards for any length of time?'

'A few years. I think we purchased the site in 2014.' He looked at the man beside him, folding the plans, and received a confirming nod.

'Looks to be quite a lot of work. A substantial investment is it?'

'I don't undertake any other kind, Inspector,' said Gowan.

'And when you take on a project like this, how does it

come about? By that I mean, you're based in Glasgow – how do you judge a place like rural Ayrshire to be ripe for development?'

'Sometimes it's about keeping your eye out for the main chance, but when you're a little more established the opportunities come knocking too.'

'And on this occasion, did opportunity knock?'

'I can't quite recall.'

Valentine reached out to the roof of the Jaguar and brushed away a stray mud speck. 'That's very interesting. You see, the former owner of Ardinsh Farm up there, he says you more or less made him an offer he couldn't refuse.'

Gowan put his hands in the pockets of his overcoat. 'I really don't remember.'

Valentine nodded and then turned back the way he had come. 'If you remember, Mr Gowan, perhaps you'd be good enough to call the station and let my team know.' He halted. 'It's a murder we're investigating, by the way.'

'It's got nothing to do with me. I just bought the land. I didn't look for any bodies first.'

'Of course you didn't. I'm merely trying to give you an indication of the gravity of the situation we're dealing with here. And, of course, an explanation for why I'll need to ask you and your men to vacate the immediate area for the time being.'

'You can't be serious.'

'Like I said, murder's a very serious business, Mr Gowan.'

16

DI Bob Valentine stood outside the chief superintendent's office, worrying the thick, brown, industrial carpet tiles so much that he guessed a static shock was imminent. He put the nerves down to the conversation he had had with Clare that morning. Much as he sympathised with his wife, and wanted to do his best for her and his family, wanted to please everyone and subjugate any considerations he might have for himself, he knew she was wrong to put him in this position.

He understood his wife's reasoning; he could even see that she had his best interests at heart, but he knew she hadn't thought about the wider consequences. He didn't, by this stage, care about the thousands of pounds they were in debt over the new extension and Clare's credit cards. They were just numbers on pieces of paper; he was over the initial shock of being poorer now than when he started his career and had come to live with it. After all, wasn't the entire country broke? Save for a few well-heeled bankers and those at the centre of power, everyone was struggling.

The thing that really worried Valentine was the job; especially the case of the two murdered schoolboys he was currently in charge of. He knew his health was fragile, both mental and physical, and he knew that was where Clare's focus was, but he also knew there was no one else on the force that could do what he did.

Valentine's experience had brought him to an understanding of the job that he was sure few shared. He didn't express this egotistically, or in any way that might indicate he had a higher regard for himself than others. What he did know, what existed at the core of him, was his self. He was a hunter – that was why he was here; there was nothing else he knew with such certainty. He was the one tasked with treading the thin blue line the papers liked to talk about. Of course there were others like him, but it was a finite supply. Who would do his job if he left? Who would find justice for those two little boys then?

He was preparing to knock as the door swung open. Standing there was the chief super and a figure so rarely seen that his appearance was a surprise to the DI.

'Ah, Bob, we were just coming to get you,' said CS Martin. 'Perfect timing.'

Chief Constable Bill Greaves extended an open hand towards Valentine. 'Hello again, Bob.'

'Sir.' He took the hand. It felt cold and limp.

'How's everything with the . . .' Greaves ran fluttering fingertips above his chest. 'After the accident that is.'

Valentine wanted to correct him: he was stabbed in the heart and it was no accident. 'Fine, sir. All mended now.'

'Good, glad to hear it. You gave us all a bit of a fright there for a little while.'

The DI accepted the concern graciously, but he knew any fright felt by Greaves or the super related only to the force's clear-up rates. If either of them truly valued his service to the force, and not just his record, then they would have left him to semi-retirement at the training college in Tulliallan. The thought mixed with Clare's earlier comments, and even earlier remarks along similar lines, and hardened Valentine's resolve.

'Come in then, Bob. We need to talk about the boys-in-the-barrel case,' said CS Martin.

Valentine felt pounced upon by his senior officers; he tried to readjust his temperament towards open-mindedness because he knew that was the only way he was going to get through the coming encounter. It was unusual, with the station's current workload, to see the chief super taking an overt interest in any one case, but to see the chief constable deigning to grace the below-stairs ranks with his presence was close to a shock.

The chief constable positioned himself behind CS Martin's desk. For a brief, comical moment Martin stood beside him looking clueless, and then something like initiative sparked behind her eyes as she turned to Valentine and edged her backside on to the corner of the desk.

'Quite an unusual occurrence,' said the chief. 'Can't remember another one like it.'

Valentine nodded. 'It's certainly the worst I've seen.'

He nodded sagely. 'Marion and myself have been discussing . . . things.'

'Things, sir?'

'We're both of the opinion that this is likely to be a spotlight case.'

The term was more police jargon that grated with Valentine. It meant a case with a lot of media interest – or, to be more specific, a lot of media interference and even more interference from the top ranks.

'I'm sure the human element will be exploited by the press in due course.'

'Indeed. It's important that we're ready for that eventuality when it raises its head.'

He had dealt with prying journalists in the past and it did not frighten him. His concern was more for the families of the victims when they identified the boys; press intrusion had a way of isolating the worst-affected individuals and making the experience as unpleasant as possible for them.

'Sir, my team is well versed in the tricks of the press. You have nothing to fear there.'

Greaves turned his gaze to Martin and leaned back in his chair, lacing his fingers over the brightly polished buttons on his chest.

'Bob, the chief constable has some concerns relating to past events with the press on your squad.'

Valentine was blindsided. He knew at once what she was referring to, but he didn't expect that to be cast up now, or used as something to attack him with. There was an angle being worked, but the DI couldn't see it.

'Rossi is back working in the family ice-cream business now. I hardly see how he's relevant to my current investigation.'

'Calm down, Bob,' said CS Martin, 'we're just making sure all the bases are covered.'

Valentine didn't get a chance to answer, adding a couple of beeps to his racing pulse.

'We need to make you aware how sensitive the issue is, Bob, that's all,' said Greaves.

The DI took a deep breath. 'Yes, sir.'

'We have to be sure that everything is shipshape and Bristol fashion on your squad, if you know what I mean.'

'You've made me aware of your concerns, sir, but I really do not believe it's an issue.'

'You see, Bob, that kind of response could be deemed complacency by some people – or worse, hubris.'

'The only pride I have is for the job. If I can make a point here, whilst we're harking back to the events of a couple of years ago, it was me who uncovered Rossi's less-than-wholesome relationship with the press, and it was me that showed him the door pending the full internal investigation. I took no chances, and I'm quite sure I'd do the same again.'

The chief constable unlaced his fingers and sprang forward in his chair. He seemed to be assessing Valentine's reaction through slitted eyes, but there was no way of telling what was going on behind the inscrutable gaze. 'OK, Bob. If you tell me your team is watertight, I'll respect your integrity.'

'Thank you, sir.'

'I'll say this though – you and I both know the kind of attention this case is going to attract from all areas of the media, and I don't just mean the *Ayrshire Post* and a few struggling nationals. This case has the potential to be an international sensation.'

Valentine winced at the chief constable's word choice. 'I understand.'

'I'm going to appoint you a direct media-liaison officer, and I'd like her to be accommodated within your squad and become an integral part of the set-up.'

'We have Colleen, sir. Are you sure that this is necessary?'

'Colleen and the press office have their hands full as

it is. No, my mind's set on this. I'll be sending you Charlotte Stubbs from Edinburgh HQ. She was a legal eagle before she became a parliamentary press secretary. She's extremely savvy and just what you need.'

If there was a backhanded insult in the chief constable's remarks Valentine let it go, in much the same way as he understood he would have to let go of any objections he might have to bringing a complete stranger into his squad.

'We'll make Charlotte feel at home, sir. If that's what you'd like.'

Greaves smiled, indicating the floor was now open to the chief super. 'Anything to add, Marion?'

'I know this must sound a bit belt and braces, Bob, but we can't be too careful,' she said.

'Of course.'

'And I'd like you to think of Charlotte as your first point of contact for the press. Anything you need to release goes through her, and I mean anything – I don't want so much as a good morning given to the hacks unless it's been written down and approved by Charlotte first.'

The DI immediately saw that this was an impossible task to ask of him. He needed the press to work with him not against him. So much of their relationship depended on *quid pro quo* that he foresaw a strategy of withholding everything might have the opposite to the desired effect. But he also saw their minds were set and he wasn't going to be stupid enough to disagree.

'We'll do it your way, boss.' He was tempted to add, 'And when it all goes tits up, I'll try not to say I told you so,' but he kept his thoughts to himself and headed back to the incident room to share the news with his team.

17

Jim Prentice was smacking the side of the vending machine and scowling when Valentine turned the corner on his way from the chief super's office.

'Lovely language for a man of your advancing years,' said Valentine. He was trying to conceal his feelings about the meeting he'd just left by dipping into banter with the desk sergeant, but he suspected his real motives were on show.

'It bloody well gave me tea when I was after coffee!'

'Give Dino a knock. She's got her own percolator in there. Might even give you a couple of digestives to put on the side.'

Prentice laughed. 'No danger. I see Jimmy Greaves is up.'

'Don't remind me. I've just pressed the flesh with the bold Greavsie.'

'Oh aye. And why are we being treated to his company? Rare as hobby-horse manure that is.'

Valentine watched Prentice wincing at the taste of the tea as he sipped from the plastic cup. 'Put it this way,' he said, 'that's the face I made too.'

'Be the barrel-boys case, no doubt. Twitchy, is he?'

'Assigned me a media specialist, for my own use. She's coming down from Edinburgh.'

'Colleen'll be chuffed.'

'It can't put her nose any more out of joint than mine. It's a bit of an unnecessary extravagance if you ask me.'

'I'd have to agree, in these straightened times and all that. Did you put him right?'

'You're joking aren't you?' snapped Valentine. 'I've just put the SOCOs on double time at the crime scene. I wouldn't have a leg to stand on.'

Prentice grinned. 'Have to go some way to beat the time you had all those uniforms bagging up the contents of the tip . . . would love to have been a fly on the wall when Dino found out. Or even just a fly on the tip!'

Valentine grinned along with the desk sergeant, but inwardly he was beginning to wonder if he had actually earned a reputation for being profligate with resources and cavalier with the press. He didn't like to question himself, especially his abilities on the job – and more so when he was engaged in a case which required high levels of confidence to get anything done – but the thought had been implanted, and he knew he'd return to it. Clare had already sown doubts about the job in his mind, and he wondered how many more he could accommodate.

'So Greavsie and Dino are in panic mode?' said Prentice.

'I don't know, Jim. Between you and me, I found the whole situation very strange. I mean for Greavsie to turn up out the blue means either I'm on the watch list or Dino is. I don't see him keeping that close an eye on our daily caseload, do you?'

'I haven't heard anything to that effect. But if you

consider that nonsense with Rossi and then there was Flash Harris filling his pockets, you can see their thinking.'

'But Harris wasn't part of my team.'

'He was working the same case, Bob.'

'It was Dino that put him on that, not me.'

'I'm only saying, mate.' Prentice creased his brows; he looked like he was readying himself to fend off another attack.

'Sorry, Jim. I must be getting jumpy.'

'It's all right, we all are. The job's not what it used to be.'

'You can say that again.'

'At my age the alternative's just as bad though. I don't fancy a night watchman's number on some building site, getting my skull stoved in for a stack of breeze blocks. It makes you wonder, doesn't it?'

'Wonder what?'

'What it's all for, if it's been worthwhile?'

Valentine looked into the desk sergeant's face; he'd done the job for more years than Valentine and he was a good desk sergeant. He had some room for bitterness, having sat all the inspector's exams and never got the break to leave uniform. It was unfair, but so was life, thought Valentine. He didn't want to ever be in Jim Prentice's position, holding on to the job for the wrong reasons. Holding out for the pension and the gold watch. That wasn't what the DI was about – the plaudits were never part of the reward for him. The politics of the station meant less than nothing to Valentine. But he knew the workings of the place and how the machinations in the ranks could interfere with the real work. He wondered if he had the heart for any more of it.

'Look, I have to go and see how the squad's getting on,

break the news to them too, Jim. Can I ask you to give me a nod if you hear anything about this new media-relations woman arriving?'

'Sure. What's her name? I'll ask for the SP with the Embra lads. Some of them are all right, don't play the old school-tie trick.'

'Stubbs – Charlotte, I think.'

'Sounds powsh.'

'It's Edinburgh, isn't it?'

'Come with a pan-loaf accent as well, I'll bet. Mind you, beats a fur coat and nae nickers, I suppose.'

Valentine grinned. 'Don't let DS McCormack hear you saying that. Very passionate about the Dear Green Place, so she is.'

Prentice turned. 'I'll catch you later, Bob.'

Valentine nodded, dismissing the offer of a cup of tea from the vending machine as the desk sergeant made a show of tipping the grey liquid into the nearest waste bin.

The incident room thrummed with activity as the DI entered. Fewer heads rose above keyboards and desktops now; the squad was too busy with the minutiae of the case. Valentine tried to clear his thoughts, to forget the conversation he'd just had with the chief super and the chief constable. He pushed away Jim Prentice's comments and analysis too, because it would only lead to distraction from the job at hand.

The DI approached the centre of the long wall that dissected the room from the rest of the floor. At the whiteboard, Donnelly had been busy posting photographs from the crime scene and further along, on an office desk shoved against the wall, the main exhibits from the bagged evidence sat out.

The detective scanned the photographs as he passed, but his attention was on the items in clear plastic bags. The boys' boots and shoes. Items of clothing, some of them filthy, muddied, but others with bright patches that stuck out like obscure, inexplicable highlights.

Valentine reached down for the smallest of the bags, a tiny item, sealed with a white sticker that looked outsized by comparison. In the bag, the detective saw the small silver St Christopher that had been retrieved from inside the oil drum where the boys had been buried.

It was a dull, unpolished item, the markings on its reverse – the initials C. B. S. – visible by the blackness of their centres. He removed the label and tipped out the contents into the palm of his hand. He held the pendant up to the light, between thumb and forefinger, and proceeded to turn it from front to back in slow succession. C. B. S. Were they one of the boys' initials? They must have meant something for someone to inscribe them on the back.

'C. B. S.,' said Valentine. He looked at the St Christopher, small, slightly misshapen, and battle-scarred with scratches and dirt. He could see nothing that spoke to him, but he felt something.

It was a strange sensation, almost a direct communication without words. As he gripped the little piece of silver in the palm of his hand the DI felt calm – far calmer than he had all morning, perhaps in days.

He knew someone would have something to say about it – it was theft after all – but he didn't care as he slipped the small silver St Christopher into his jacket pocket and tapped the outside seam to make sure it was in there.

The doubts he held about the job didn't seem to matter

any more. What mattered was those boys – those nameless children that he had sworn to find some kind of justice for. After what they had seen, and what they'd been through, Valentine knew there was no justice to be found that could possibly mean anything to them. They'd lived and inhabited a world that had forsaken them and one that he was growing to despise, but finding justice and letting them rest in peace was all he could do for them. And he would do it.

18

September 1982

I don't know how it happened, it just did.

I don't want anyone to know. I'm trying to be quiet about it, but the floorwalker has found out.

'What's this, Welsh?' he says.

I don't answer, just stand there, but he sees me shivering and pulls back the blankets.

'You've pissed the bed, you little bastard.' He slaps me. The sound of the crack on my head echoes in the room, and I duck away to avoid the second blow. But I'm too slow.

'Ah, leave it!' I shout out. There's boys mumbling now – they know what's happened. I want to run or find something hard to hit the floorwalker with. He yells again, but I don't hear the words, just feel the grip of his hand on my neck, the fat fingers digging into my flesh. The pain of it is making it difficult to walk. I have to go up on tiptoes and he drags me along, into the bathroom.

The floorwalker sticks my head in the toilet bowl and pulls the chain. He holds me there, and I wonder will I drown, but then he yanks me out and I gulp deep breaths.

That's when I see the others; the boys are gathered at the door – silent, watching.

'Piss the bed, eh?' he yells.

I vomit now. A little at first, just on my nightshirt, and then more splashes on the toilet-room floor. I'm smacked again, on the head, and again, in the stomach this time. I fall over and land on my hands and knees.

'Pick it up!'

'What with, I have nothing.'

'Your bloody hands or your mouth, I don't care which.' He plants his boot on my backside and I fall into the vomit, and that's when I feel more of it coming. I grab the rim of the bowl and retch loudly.

'You little . . .' The floorwalker grabs my head and pushes it into the toilet bowl again. There's my vomit in there, floating in the water. The smell of it makes me sick once more. I hear the boys jeering.

'Get back to your pits, there's not one among you that isn't liable to this sort of performance.' He takes a short step towards the boys, one hand raised over his head, and they scatter.

I'm out the water now, resting and gathering my breath on the floor. I'm soaked through and stinking of my vomit.

'On your feet.'

I stand up and I see even my feet are wet.

'Mop up that mess – now.'

'I've no mop.'

'With your hands, you fool.'

I kneel down and try to scoop up my sick with my hands. It escapes through the gaps in my fingers and runs down my arms. There's fuller bits, undigested lumps of lamb from the broth we had earlier, and I pick those up with my fingertips as he watches. There's still some there, some sick, when he says give it a wipe with my sleeve. My nightshirt is filthy smelly.

'Right. Wait here. Don't move.'

The floorwalker returns with a tin pail and there's a wooden handle sticking out the top. He takes a bottle of powdered bleach and tips some in the pail. There's water there and it mixes.

'Clean this floor. Every inch of it.'

I take the mop and do as he says. The water and the bleach splash on my feet and legs and it stings me. It's still stinging when I've mopped the whole floor and there's grey water running down the gutter at the middle of the tiles and into the drain that gurgles.

'Are you done?'

I nod.

He grabs the pail from me and turns it on its side. I see the grey water with the bleach in it as he sprays it over my legs. It splashes on to my knees and thighs and wets the hem of my nightshirt. The smell makes me feel sick again but I swallow it down.

'Stand in the corridor – go on.'

I walk out to the dormitory, through the heavy doors, and into the brightly lit corridor. It's cold but I stand by the great iron radiator that reaches my shoulder.

'Not there, in the middle of the floor.'

I walk away to the middle of the floor, under the glare of the white light. My eyes are stinging with the brightness of it, but my legs are stinging more. They're pink-red now like the colour of the pork sides hanging in the kitchen freezer.

I feel as cold as that pork too, shivering where I stand in a shrill draft that blows under the door.

The floorwalker turns the knob on the radiator to off and says, 'Don't you move. Don't you dare move until the morning. Do you hear me?'

I nod at him but say nothing. I think I want to kill him as he points the broom handle at me and says, 'I'll teach you to piss the bed again. See how a week sleeping out here suits you.'

He makes me sleep there all week. And for weeks after, every night, I'm woken with other boys who have pissed the bed once and made to queue up to use the toilet. Those who don't perform to order are not allowed back to their beds but have to sleep on one of the bentwood chairs, back in the corridor.

I'll never wet the bed again. I know that for sure.

19

The Carrick Lodge occupied the no man's land where the exclusivity of Alloway gave way to the town of Ayr. The road from the tiny shack-like cottage of the poet Robert Burns to the tip of town was lined with the kinds of properties overpaid company heads aspired to. When Valentine was a boy, the homes here were occupied by an Ayrshire royalty that no longer seemed to exist. Celebrities like low-grade television presenters and the odd ersatz country and western singer had long since sold up and moved on, leaving the elegant driveways and backyard swimming pools to a new breed of parvenu.

It seemed a strange place for a man of the people like Davie Purves to want to meet but when he thought about it Valentine conceded the logic was about right for an ex-cop. The Carrick Lodge was located right at the end of the Maybole Road, with simple enough access to the A77 and all roads back to Cumnock. It was also far enough away from the former mining town to be out of the range of prying eyes. As a further caution, nobody that Purves mixed with at home was ever likely to be a golfer – that was a role for the assuredly middle class and those confident enough of their retired status to be able to dress in Argyle sweaters and lemon-coloured slacks.

In the bar Valentine located Purves in the corner of the room: every cop's favourite spot because of the view it afforded. The DI approached and introduced DS McCormack, a move which at first seemed to annoy Purves but he thawed somewhat under the full beam of McCormack's smile.

'There weren't many women of your rank outside of *Prime Suspect* in my day,' said Purves.

McCormack grinned. 'I doubt I live up to Helen Mirren on close inspection.'

Valentine extended a hand towards Purves. 'Hello, Davie. That you reminiscing about the old days already?'

'I notice you didn't say the good old days,' said Purves.

'I'm choosing my words carefully. Nice to see you.'

Valentine left McCormack with the retired cop and placed an order at the bar. On his return they were talking about the Old Firm and bonding over Glasgow Rangers' recent return to the Premiership.

The DI kept his footballing allegiance to himself and waited for the coffees to arrive before bringing the conversation round to why he had asked to see Purves. The details of the case, laid bare by Valentine, didn't seem to shock the former detective as much as it had everyone else, but Valentine put this down to a mock show of bravado.

'I can honestly say, Bob, that I remember nothing like that from my time on the force,' said Purves.

'No. I wasn't expecting you to. I dare say if there was anything even close to resembling two boys murdered and dumped in a barrel we'd all have heard of it.'

'So how can I help?'

'In any way you can, Davie. We're at sixes and sevens on this one.'

'Any persons of interest?'

'One.' Valentine looked at McCormack.

'Bloke by the name of Garry Keirns,' said the DS.

Purves nodded. 'Of course. Ardinsh Farm isn't it? Makes sense.'

'You know him?'

'Oh yeah, everybody in the town knows about Keirns. He's a piece of shit but I'd put murder beyond him. Petty theft and small-time drug dealing's more his line. I think we done him for a car-stereo racket once as well, had dozens of them up at Sandy Thompson's place. Poor bugger, Sandy. Must have saw Keirns far enough.'

'What do you mean?' said Valentine.

'It's common knowledge that Keirns diddled him out of that farm, what was left of it like. Sandy had been selling off parcels of land for years to meet debts.'

'Whose debts – Sandy's or Keirns's?'

Purves tasted his coffee and started to add more sugar. 'Does it matter? Sandy was the one paying them out. By that stage he was well into drink and more besides.'

'I'd heard a whisper that Keirns was his facilitator.'

'Christ, is that what they're calling it now, Bob? Keirns virtually poured the drink down Sandy's neck and shoved a few pills there too. You don't need to believe what folk say, Bob. I saw it first-hand.'

'You did?'

Purves seemed content with his coffee now, smiling as he placed it back on the table. 'I was one of the team tailing him when he was done for growing the cannabis out at the farm.'

Valentine interrupted. 'I didn't see anything about that on his sheet.'

'No, he wriggled out of it in the end. Had a very good lawyer from Edinburgh. Don't ask me how he paid for it. He had some connections, even had a character reference from an MP. The judge threw the case out. Look, he's dodgy – you can take my word for it. As I was saying when I was on the tail team I saw him buying bottles every night for Sandy. He must have been funnelling it down the poor old bastard's neck. But murder, no way. Keirns wouldn't have the guts for that.'

The DI played over Purves's comments and looked at McCormack to check her for an opinion. He didn't need to ask; her expression indicated a similar amount of curiosity with the revelations. On one level, they were no further forward, but Purves had suggested some interesting possibilities.

'How does a scrote like Keirns get the support of local worthies?' said Valentine.

'You tell me. Was it the drugs? Maybe he was supplying some of the upper-class party set.'

'That wouldn't be enough for them to stick their necks out for him,' said McCormack.

'No, it wouldn't. But it would be enough for Keirns to use for blackmail,' said Valentine.

Purves nodded. 'Exactly. And that is not the kind of caper I'd put past Garry Keirns. In fact, I'd say it was right up his street.'

Valentine assessed the retired cop's words and presented another query that was forming in his mind. 'But where did Keirns get access to that sort of people? He didn't move in those circles, did he?'

'I suppose that's where the boys' clubs come in, the

charity work for Columba House,' said Purves. 'Look at the *Chronicle* from a few years back. Keirns was never out the paper for some fundraiser or other. Used to get backs up at the station to see Keirns handing over an outsized cheque to some councillor or other that was supplying new footy tops for Columba House. We knew Keirns must be working a scam, we just never knew how.'

'That makes sense – Keirns was an ex-Columba boy himself,' said Valentine.

'I dare say he milked it for all it was worth, played the poor orphan card with all those local worthies.'

'I'm getting a pretty good picture of him now, Davie. You've been a big help.'

Purves reached for his overcoat on the back of the chair. 'I don't want to give you the wrong idea, Bob. Garry Keirns is as immoral as they come. He's a scrote too, but he's spineless. If you're looking for someone capable of killing kiddies, Keirns hasn't got the bottle.'

'I hear you, Davie,' said Valentine. 'Can I ask one more favour?'

Purves was fastening his overcoat. 'Name it.'

'That character reference Keirns had from the MP, can you remember who it was from?'

He shook his head. 'Sorry. The lawyer was a big shot from Edinburgh – Armstrong was his name. Bloody QC he was. The MP was a fair age mind, he'll be retired now.'

Valentine watched McCormack take down the name of the lawyer in her notebook. 'Do you think you can ask around, maybe find out who the MP was?'

'I'll see what I can do.'

20

As DI Bob Valentine descended the stairs to the basement of King Street station he felt strangely compelled to put his hand in the pocket of his jacket. Removing the St Christopher pendant that he'd taken from the evidence bag he looked directly into his open palm.

The small item appeared to have been polished, perhaps the result of the lint in his pocket and the day's movements. It was certainly shinier as he eyed it, squinting directly under the mounted wall light. The three initials C. B. S. still baffled the detective, but the mere presence of the pendant felt comforting to him. It seemed to have an energy that spoke to the DI. He couldn't intuit any more from the piece, but he felt sure in time that he would.

As Valentine returned the pendant to his pocket and took the final steps towards the basement storage he tapped the outside of his pocket and spoke softly. 'Consider this part of the test.' He didn't know who he was speaking to, probably Crosbie seemed the closest guess, but he felt like persisting, if only because he had nothing to lose.

'Ally . . .' called out Valentine.

'Over here, boss.' DS McAlister was propped against a row of shelving that was composed of chrome and wire mesh and divided into large and small files of ascending order. At his feet more files had been stacked, some to waist height and accompanied by paper cups and takeaway wrappings from the chippie on Ayr Road.

'Christ, have you moved in here?' said Valentine.

McAlister glanced around him. 'It's tidier than my flat, sir.'

'I dread to think what Chez Ally looks like then. You must live in a bloody sewer.'

He raised his arm and sniffed at his armpits. 'Do I smell that bad?'

Valentine didn't reply. He walked towards the pile of box files on the floor and crouched down. 'Anything of use here?'

McAlister scratched his stubbled chin as he spoke. 'Don't know where to begin really. Yes and no might be a good answer to that question. Perhaps more yes than no.'

'Come on then, spill the beans.'

The DS tapped a pile of files with the toe of his shoe. 'That's the possibles pile . . .'

Valentine cut in. 'The what?'

'Possibles, sir. As in, possibly our missing boys, but not very likely.'

'OK. And the rest?'

McAlister motioned towards a smaller pile. 'Plausibles, sir. Slightly more believable than the possibles but not as hot as'—he knelt down beside the DI and tapped at a thin pile of files—'the most likely cases. That's this pile, and it's pretty slim pickings, as you can see.'

Valentine took a file from the top of the largest pile and stood up. It was difficult to read in the basement, the dim glow of the bulbs requiring some adjustment of the eyes. 'How can you read down here?'

'It's not easy.'

'How far are you from a definitive list, Ally? I mean, do I have to move a Z bed down here for you?'

McAlister shook his head. 'I'm just about done, sir. Really just double-checking I haven't missed anything.'

'So this little lot' – he motioned to the floor – 'is what we have to go on?'

'Pretty much.'

'Right. I want the pick of your three piles upstairs within the hour. Is that doable?'

'I don't see why not. I can always return if we don't get anything. That will need some serious excavation though. I think I've got all that's graspable. I mean, what's easy to lay hands on.'

'OK, Ally. Upstairs in an hour.' Valentine headed for the door and left the DS to sort out his findings. Back at his desk he checked his email account and found there was new mail from Davie Purves. The wording of the email was typically laconic, but an attachment promised more information.

Valentine clicked on the file.

As the document opened up it appeared to be some kind of a scan. It was on headed notepaper and typed with an old typewriter ribbon. As Valentine zoomed in on the header he saw it was House of Commons notepaper and immediately drew a sharp breath.

'Christ above, Davie.' Purves had supplied the MP's character statement on Garry Keirns from 12 October 1988.

122

Andrew Lucas was the siting MP for Carrick, Cumnock and Doon Valley in '88, a Labour man, but not one that Valentine had any knowledge of. His interest in politics at that time was minimal, his interest in individual politicians verging on miniscule. His father, the ex-miner, had viewed them all with disdain, and his opinions had been transmitted, unfiltered, to his son.

The DI read the letter from Lucas, homing in on individual phrases: community minded; hard-working; asset to the town and district; no hesitation in endorsing this young man of the strongest character and utmost sensibility.

'I see why you got off, Garry.'

Valentine took the letter into the incident room and pinned it on the board.

'What's that?' said McCormack, looking up.

'Read it and weep.'

The DS rose from her desk and approached the board. It took her less than a minute to see through the missive. 'Is this Lucas having a laugh?'

'Doesn't ring true to our Garry Keirns, does it?'

'Not one iota. Jesus, makes you wonder what Keirns was paying him.'

DS Donnelly's interest was stirred by the latest addition to the board. He was pushing back his chair as DS McAlister walked in the room. 'By the holy . . . Robinson Crusoe returns!'

'Right, everyone,' yelled Valentine. 'Can I have your attention round here? Ally has some interesting discoveries to pass on.'

'I hope this is a demonstration of how to light a fire with

two sticks,' said Donnelly. 'I always wondered how to do that.'

McAlister grimaced as he placed the files on the table under the whiteboard.

'Fire away, son,' said Valentine. 'Sorry, you know what I mean.'

The DS constructed his three piles in front of the team. 'Right, I'll try to keep this simple, for the likes of Phil.'

'Funny,' said Donnelly.

McAlister continued. 'The cold cases we have downstairs from the early to mid-eighties are all a bit of a jumble, but there are a few of interest. I separated those into the possible, plausible and most likely.'

'Which is the big pile, Ally?' said McCormack.

'Our least likely, I'm afraid. That one consists of cases from throughout the country with ties to Cumnock and Ayrshire. We had two prominent serial killers operating at this time and one was a lorry driver whose regular route took him through Cumnock, almost weekly.'

Valentine raised a hand. 'You're presupposing a snatched child from elsewhere then?'

'More or less.'

'That doesn't explain the local school uniform though,' said Donnelly.

'I know. Only one of the boys is in St John's garb though – the other could be a snatch. I'm also allowing for the possibility that the uniform could be a plant, to throw police off the trail.'

The DI cut the air with his hand. 'Moving on to the next lot, Ally.'

'Yes, OK. The plausibles include three young boys that went missing from a tinker site . . .'

124

'I think we call them itinerant now, Ally,' said McCormack.

'Whatever . . . the three boys disappeared in the January of '83 and by the Feb we were getting unconfirmed sightings of them in the Irish Republic, but they were never followed up properly. The one time we got the Gardaí to do a proper recce of the site they were spotted at, everyone had moved on. I think it's interesting that the boys were the same age as ours – ten, eleven and twelve. I thought it was worth looking at, especially as the ten-year-old attended St John's for a while, though it was only a matter of weeks and, being a tinker's kid, not likely in uniform.'

Valentine removed a chair from the desk he was standing over and lowered himself into it. He sat with his head resting on the flat of his hand as he spoke again. 'I'm hoping the most-likely file is better than what you've shown us so far, Ally.'

'I'm coming to that now, sir. This was quite a high-profile disappearance going by the records. Two young lads, local boys from Cumnock, who went missing in 1984. That's exactly thirty-two years ago, sir, so fits our pathology profile of the boys in the oil drum precisely.'

'Now we're getting somewhere a little more promising. Go on, Ally.'

McAlister hovered over the open file, seeming unsure of where to begin to present the information he'd accumulated. 'Well, the case got a lot of press, even made the nightly news regularly because there were a lot of child disappearances then.'

Donnelly spoke, nodding. 'Yeah, there were a number of

prominent serial killers we know about now that we didn't then.'

McCormack agreed. 'And the year before we've just had those three boys we thought might be sighted in Ireland.'

'Yeah,' said McAlister, 'we've got a lot of pressure on to find these boys . . . but nothing.'

'Nothing?' said Valentine.

'Disappeared off the face of the earth, sir. Two boys, both local and still unaccounted for.'

'Names?'

'Donal Welsh and Rory Stevenson.'

The DI pushed back his chair. He felt like he'd been struck on the back of the head. 'Jesus!'

'Everything OK, sir?' said McCormack.

Valentine was clawing at his head and neck. 'Get that file up here now.'

21

Valentine let the tap run, filling his cupped hands with cold water. He could hear DS McCormack knocking on the door and calling his name but he had already decided to ignore her. As he splashed the water on his face he shivered a little, the coldness coming as a shock but not sufficient to knock out his nausea. The skin on his face felt warm to the touch and was burning on his neck and at the base of his skull.

'Bob, will you open up in there?' McCormack knocked on the door again.

The DI knew he would have to answer her sooner or later; he'd left the incident room in too much of a hurry for her not to notice that something wasn't right. He was about to call back and send her on her way when the retching started.

The involuntary contraction in Valentine's stomach signalled to his throat, and he folded towards the sink. He hoped the noise of the running tap would drown out the dry vomiting, but he knew at once it hadn't. The detective was bent over, supporting himself on one knee when McCormack eased through the door.

'Sir, let's get you on your feet.' She rushed around him, fretting.

'Sylvia, this is the Gents.'

'I know. You're burning up. On second thoughts perhaps we should sit you down.' McCormack negotiated the cubicle door behind her and tipped down the toilet seat, helping the DI to rest his weight.

'If anyone sees us like this there'll be talk.'

'Christ, there's talk as it is.'

Valentine ran the sleeve of his shirt over his wet face. 'Is there? I never hear any.'

'You're the boss, who's going to gossip to you?'

'I'll have to watch what I say now.'

McCormack laughed. 'No more overnight stays on Arran either.'

'That's not funny.'

The DS agreed with Valentine. 'Sir, you're so pale I can't tell where your shirt ends and your face begins. What's happened?'

'Nothing, just a headache.'

'Oh, come on.' She tilted her chin towards her shoulder. 'I do this for a living, remember.'

'OK, I had another turn.'

'Like the others?'

'Yes . . . and no.'

'Meaning?'

'Meaning if I close my eyes I can still see the face of the wee boy who appeared to me in the incident room.'

'What did you say?'

'I think you heard. Now, look, you need to get out of here before someone sees you.'

'I will if you will. Come on, you're going home. It's past six so you'll not be missed.'

'But . . .'

'No buts, Bob. On your feet. I can brief the team about anything that needs doing.'

The DI pushed himself off the toilet seat and steadied himself on the narrow walls of the cubicle. 'Right, you first.'

'I'll be watching the door. You go straight from here to the car park, got it?'

'I'll need my coat, the car keys are in there.'

'OK, I'll get it. Sure you're OK to drive?'

He nodded. 'Yes, as long as I keep my eyes open.'

'I find that's the best way to drive myself. I'll get your coat.'

The open window helped to cool his brows and the ache in his neck subsided. On the way to Masonhill Valentine felt himself returning to normal. The physical symptoms, though a worry, were not his greatest fear.

Since the knifing incident and the heart surgery, he didn't worry about physical injury any more. If that was truly the worst that the physical world had to offer then he knew he could take it again. There was only one thing now which frightened Valentine and that was more hurt for his family.

Clare had been the one who had taken the news of his near death the worst. She had been driven to a state of nervous exhaustion – for a woman who lived on her nerves at the best of times this was not a good place to be. He knew she had been close to the edge and that he'd been very near to losing her. He couldn't face that again.

Any pain was worth it for Valentine if it meant his wife and children were spared; it may have taken him a long time to realise this, but they were the most important things in his life. The rest, including the job he had given so much to, was meaningless without them.

'Oh my God!' Chloe's reaction to seeing her father walk through the front door was unexpected.

'No, it's only me, love.'

'But at a Christian hour – to what do we owe the pleasure?'

Valentine saw his wife through the door to the kitchen. She was wearing an apron that cinched her waist. As she approached, smiling, she wiped her fingertips on the apron. 'Bob, you're in time for dinner.'

'Is it really such a rare occurrence?'

Clare and Chloe nodded together.

'Where's Fiona?'

'Setting the table with your dad,' said Clare. 'I'll have to tell them to set an extra place now.'

The nagging guilt that Valentine had left home with in the morning came back to assault him. He knew there had been too many family meals that he'd missed, but he told himself that was going to change as he watched Clare and Chloe exchange excitement.

As the DI removed his jacket and hung it on the hallstand he felt an urge to check the pocket. The St Christopher was still there. As he held the pendant in his hand he drew a fist around it and closed his eyes for the briefest of instants. The little boy's face was still there, above a St John's school tie with a small silver pendant sitting on the knot.

'Hello, Rory,' whispered Valentine; he felt he was going to be seeing a lot more of him now.

At dinner the DI laughed and joked with his family. He had forgotten how warm and intimate these occasions could be. Had he really denied himself this simple pleasure for so long? He had been wrong and Clare had been right, he saw that, and he knew he must do something about it. But there was a new ache in his heart too, for the two young boys who had been deprived of their lives too soon. As much as he felt responsible to his family, Valentine felt responsible for those boys too.

'Leave the dishes, Clare. I'll get those.'

'I could get used to this,' she said.

'Trust me, love, you will.'

Valentine shooed his wife and the girls into the living room and press-ganged his father into clearing up the dinner dishes.

'If you don't mind, Dad?' he said.

'Doesn't bother me, I was always a worker.'

When they were alone, with only the sound of the dishes rattling, Valentine spoke again. 'Can I ask you about someone from the old place?'

'Cumnock?'

'Yeah. His name cropped up on this case I'm working.'

'Those two wee boys?' His father shook his head.

'Yes, that one.'

'Who is it?'

'A politician, name of Lucas.'

'Andy Lucas, the Labour man?'

'That's him. Do you know him?'

'Not now – he's long gone. Died at the tail end of the eighties, I think. What do you want to know about him for – or shouldn't I ask?'

Valentine dipped another plate in the sink. 'His name came up, that's all. He gave a reference, in glowing terms, for Garry Keirns.'

'Did he now?'

'Does that surprise you?'

'Nothing those bastards do surprises me. There'll be a motive behind it, mind you. Andy Lucas wasn't a man to trade favours for nowt – he was a bloody taker who'll not be forgotten in Cumnock.'

'How do you mean?'

His father put down the dishcloth. 'The town made Lucas. He had the biggest majority in the country. He was backed by every striking miner in the place because he was seen as our man, he was Labour like, but he let us all down badly when he walked away after the strike was lost.'

'Why did he walk away?'

'You tell me. Like I say he had the biggest majority in the country in that seat – he could have been sitting pretty for the rest of his days, but he ditched us all' – he started to wring the dishtowel in his hands – 'and look who we got in his place – bloody Gerry Fallon. It took a lot more to knock that bastard off the gravy train.'

'He's retired now, Fallon, isn't he?'

'Oh, aye, he was one of the New Labour mob. They're all retired now, aren't they? With their gilt-edged pensions and their investment-bank jobs. Make you bloody sick.'

The door from the living room opened up. 'I don't see much impact being made on those dishes,' said Clare.

'Och, we're gabbin', as usual!' said the older man.

'Well when you're finished, a cup of tea would be nice.'

Valentine nodded. 'Yes, dear. Any more orders just fire away.'

22

Jim Prentice was sorting out the mail when Valentine appeared at the door of King Street station.

'Morning, Bob,' Prentice called out, summoning the DI with a conspiratorial wink.

'How do, Jim?'

'I'm fine. It's you I'm worried about.'

Valentine leaned on the counter. 'Oh, aye . . .'

'Your new team player isn't a player at all.'

'What?'

'Charlotte Stubbs. I checked her out with the Edinburgh craft.'

'Jesus, Jim, I thought you were going to keep it under your hat.'

'Those boys are sound as a pound. Anyway, she's not on the team so to speak, but she's got no shortage of supporters among the top brass. Her media experience is precisely zip from what I can go on. She was a lawyer, but for some reason she gets flown about a lot.'

'I bloody knew it. So she's snooping on us?'

'Looks that way,' said Prentice, fastening a stray shirt button. 'Any ideas why?'

'No – well none more than the usual. I've had too many loose canons on my squad lately.'

'Might be related, might not. Could it be Greavsie's got the jitters?'

'About what? I'm working a cold case that's thirty-two years old. Hardly anything there likely to come and bite him on the arse.'

'You never know. Look, take it easy anyway, eh . . . I can see this news has rattled you.'

'It's not that, Jim. I've not been myself since the stabbing, and Clare's been at me to ease up. We had a lovely family evening last night, dinner together, sat in front of the telly.' He looked up from his memory. 'You see where I'm coming from, don't you?'

'You put in more hours than Big Ben. I'm surprised this hasn't occurred to you before.'

Valentine stepped back from the counter. 'Catch you later, Jim.'

On his way up the stairs the DI felt his promising mood evaporate to be replaced by a burning temper. He had got as far as closing the door of Incident Room One when it was flung open again by the chief super. He still had one arm in his jacket as she approached with a bellicose glower beaming from her eyes.

'What the hell are you doing with the Cumnock site?' She levelled her voice, but it was still louder than usual.

'Excuse me?' said Valentine.

'I'm just off the phone to some arsehole called Gowan . . .'

'Ah, Freddie Gowan. He's an arsehole all right.' The DI hung up his coat and headed for his office at the other end of the long room.

'And why is he calling me at this hour, ranting and raving about time being money and calling in his lawyers?'

Valentine sat behind his desk and booted up his computer. 'He won't get far, chief. He's trying to build a road over my murder site. Last time I checked we were within our rights to shut him down pending an investigation.'

The chief super folded her arms before the desk; her tone had lowered in volume, if not in its intensity. She had not picked a good day to mount her attack on DI Valentine. 'And you thought that was wise, did you? Especially after our chat with the chief constable.'

'Wisdom didn't come into it. It's procedure, and I'd shut down Gowan's roadworks before we spoke.'

A long red fingernail was drawn in front of the DI and pointed, threateningly. 'I'm not sure I like your tone, Bob.'

'I'm not sure I care. I have two dead boys, mummified in a bloody barrel. If you have another detective inspector you think is better qualified than me to deal with that, and who'd be happy to have the chief constable's Mata Hari seconded to his team, then by all means let's talk about my transfer.'

The chief super withdrew her finger and refolded her arms. 'Am I hearing right, Bob?'

'Yesterday my wife told me she was leaving me if I didn't ask for a move from the murder squad. I was on my way to your office to ask just that when you presented me with the chief constable's press manoeuvre.'

'Oh, I see. And I presume you're serious about this transfer?'

'Deadly. In fact, you can consider this my formal request if you like.'

135

'Well, consider it denied. You know what the staffing situation is like in here. If it wasn't bad enough we just lost DI Harris to early retirement, and I don't see a replacement on the horizon. No, you're going bloody nowhere, Bob.'

'Well, I asked.'

'And the answer's no. And it'll still be no if you ask tomorrow.'

Valentine stood up. 'I'll put my request in writing to the chief constable in that case.'

'*What*? I don't believe I'm hearing this.'

'We have a strong lead on one of the victims. I'd anticipate having the boy ID'd properly in a matter of days. I'll hold on to the letter until I clear this one up, unless my wife finds out, but don't worry, I won't leave you in the lurch.'

The chief super's face had set firm; only her eyes followed Valentine as he walked towards the office door.

'I'm about to debrief the team, chief. You're welcome to sit in if you like,' said Valentine.

Martin's jaw tensed at its edges. She looked to be biting down hard as she stomped for the door and grabbed the handle. 'We'll talk later, Bob.'

'Yes, chief.'

DS McCormack and DS Donnelly were making their way to Valentine's office as the chief super breezed past them. McCormack turned down the corners of her mouth as she entered the small office. 'Was it something you said, sir?'

'You better believe it,' said Valentine. 'Right, Sylvia, you've been dealing with Freddie Gowan's office, haven't you?'

'Yes, on and off.'

'Well, you're back on. Find out where he is this morning and bring him in.'

'Bring him in, sir?'

'Tell him you'll charge him with obstructing a police investigation if he gives you any bother. I'm sick of pussy-footing around him and Garry Keirns.'

'OK, sir. I'll get right on that.'

'And, Phil, I want you to bring in Keirns today too. Preferably at exactly the same time as Sylvia brings in Gowan. If they see each other on the way in, it might prompt them to think about actually telling us what we want to know. It's time to start tightening the thumbscrews.'

23

Valentine took the seat he was directed to by the lab's receptionist and waited for a familiar face to materialise. There had been messages left on his phone from the SOCOs on site at Ardinsh Farm and a growing stack of yellow Post-it notes stuck on his desk by the squad, but he wanted to get the final assessments first-hand.

The boffins had a way of detailing their findings in entirely antiseptic language that was prone to missing the salient points. It took a special skill to decipher the lab reports, and Valentine had found it was often best to go straight to the source.

Much of what was coming in now was already old news to the DI: the results on the tie and the ICI drum were a foregone conclusion, but he still had some questions to ask about the other items that he had seen bagged and listed in the catalogue of crime-scene contents.

As he waited in the reception area Valentine tried not to be influenced by the pacing white coats he could see beyond the window. The Glasgow lab was a clinical place and not somewhere the DI liked to dwell for any length of time. Even the chair he sat in, though a sofa, was rigid. The whole place felt stiff, like no one had ever managed to make the interior feel familiar.

At the station, even at the morgue, there were little indicators of human existence: potted plants, picture frames on desks and the occasional bumper-sticker philosophy posted on a wall. None of that existed here in the cold, white space where people passed each other unsmiling and seemingly engrossed in their own importance.

Valentine occupied himself with the listings of items recovered from the barrel alongside the two boys. Now that he felt almost certain of the victims' identities, it was possible to attach some of the property to each individual. He drew up a list and ticked off what he thought went where.

Rory: white shirt, elasticated school tie, long black trousers, grey V-neck sweater, Clarks' shoes, white towelling socks, white Y-fronts, white vest, leather satchel, paper jotters, Spiderman comic, Panini football stickers, Tesco carrier containing Adidas trainers, Sekonda watch.

He added one more item to the list under Rory's name – St Christopher pendant. The DI had no firm evidence to make this claim, only his instinct, but he felt sure enough of that to conclude the list with the item.

As Valentine totted up the boy's possessions and ran his index finger down the list, he felt a deepening sense of anguish for the loss of such a young life. Everything on the list spoke to Valentine in familiar tones – the football stickers, the boy's watch; everything was so prosaic, and so much reminded him of his own boyhood.

Rory was a child, just like any other. On the day he died he had gone to school, he'd carried his gym kit in his satchel.

Did he trade football stickers that day? Did he measure his time away from home on the seventeen-jewels Sekonda with the winding mechanism? It was painful to visualise the boy's final hours, but somebody had to. Somebody had to try to make sense of the way two young boys came to be murdered thirty-two years ago in the same town that Valentine had grown up in.

The DI was making his way through Donal's list, pondering over the penknife and the bookie's pen, when he heard his name called.

'Hello, Bob.' It was Mike Sullivan. He held a cardboard file which he shuffled as he reached out to greet the DI.

'Mike, how's it going?'

'Busy as a one-armed man in a wallpaper-hanging contest.'

'Welcome to my world.'

The man in the starched white coat led Valentine towards the lab door, keying in the combination on the touch pad.

'I think we're just about there with your case. It's tugged a few heart strings through here, let me tell you.'

'It's a nasty business.'

'That's putting it mildly. Any idea who did it?'

'I was hoping you could help with that.'

Sullivan frowned. 'There's not much to go on. You know we're missing the murder weapon and the ligature. The rest is just filling the gaps. I'm sorry, Bob, but I don't think there's much here of help.'

Valentine strolled up to the lab counter where some of the evidence bags were being stored. There were more bags on a slightly lower table towards the window where the sunlight was dappling the trees.

'The barrel's serial number was no good then?'

'One of nearly ten thousand distributed that month, farming pesticide. The record keeping was lost when they went on to computers. No dice, I'm afraid.'

'Oh, we cleaned up that tie though . . .' Sullivan reached over for a clear plastic bag. It was secured by a bulldog clip, the tie clearly visible inside. 'Came up not bad.'

'It's St John's all right. We have that more or less confirmed from other sources.'

'Sorry, Bob. We're not helping you out much.'

'What about the jotters, from the satchel?'

'Blank.'

'You mean not even a name on the front?'

'Unused, I'd say. We thought they might have been marked with pencil but the graphite test showed nothing up.'

'No impressions, indentations?'

'You mean on the covers? No, nothing.'

Valentine leaned on the table and looked out the window. 'It would have been nice to have something more solid, before we start presenting this stuff to family members.'

'What about that pendant?' said Sullivan.

'The initials don't match any of the names from the cold-case files. It must be for something else.' He eased himself away from the table. 'Look, if we're lucky, the site search might reveal something.'

'You haven't heard?' Sullivan turned to face the DI.

'Heard what?'

'Of course, you'd have been on the A77 getting here. Bernie called an hour ago. They have a couple of interesting finds from Ardinsh Farm.'

'Go on . . .'

141

'Well, there was an envelope beneath the floorboards of the upstairs bedroom with an old photograph in it. He seemed quite excited about the picture.'

'A picture of what?'

Sullivan's voice rose. 'Something mucky.'

'You mean sexual?'

'It appears that way. I haven't seen it though. It should be back here this afternoon. I'll scan it and send it over.'

'You do that, Mike. Soon as you can.' Valentine crossed the tiled floor, his shoes slapping the surface loudly. 'Message me on the phone when it's sent. I'll be in the interview room most likely.'

'You mean you have a suspect?'

'I wouldn't go that far. More like a person of interest.'

24

January 1983

A man in a black car comes with a bag full of football tops. All the boys are excited to see them, and a great fight breaks out over the goalie's shirt with the padded elbows. Nobody wants to be the goalie usually, but today all the boys are scrapping to stand between the sticks.

The man with the black car laughs so hard he starts a coughing fit, and the master has to slap him on the back, though I think it's all for a laugh and a joke. When the man stops coughing and lights a cigarette, I know it can't be serious, and soon he's laughing again with the master.

It's Saturday and the whole place is empty. Columba House they call it – I know that now because I hear it so many times. The cook has left thick broth the colour of peeled potatoes on the range. Two grand old pots of it, bubbling away for all to see as the boys put dibs on their football shirts.

'Aren't you having one?' the man says. He talks quietly, almost a whisper, so only I can hear.

I shrug. 'Don't mind.'

'Come on, you'll play a game of football with the rest

of the lads, surely?' He smiles at me and then the master points to the table where the boys are wrestling over the shirts.

'Join in, Donal,' he says in that posh voice he has. I do as I'm told, because I don't want to feel the switch on my backside again.

The boys run about like hooligans – there's no sense to it at all. I try to reach the ball when it comes near me, but I'm immediately swamped by the mass of boys.

'Stick in, lads,' shouts the master.

It's cold and the field is wet. The grass is far too long for sports of any kind but especially for the football. It's an old leather ball and it becomes waterlogged and so heavy that it hurts your foot when you kick it. Some of the boys hold back and try to avoid the ball, but the master tells them to get stuck in and not be afraid of the ball.

I see the man with the black car watching the boys. He's still smoking, putting the little filter tip to his thin mouth and blowing white streams of smoke into the cold air. He looks at me now and again, and there's a smile on his face for me, but I don't smile back. After a while he stops smiling altogether and looks away when I stare at him.

There's a goal. That's the fifth, or is it the sixth? I can't tell. I can hardly tell what boys are on my team with all the running around and the shouting. Some of the bigger boys get cocksure, and the master has to shout about putting them in the sin bin. I don't pay too much attention though, until it's too late.

'Donal . . . Donal . . . can you hear me?' The voice sounds strange, like he's talking through a musical instrument – a tuba or something.

'Donal . . . that was a hell of a knock you took.'

I feel like I'm underwater; my head hurts and my eye socket feels numb, and then I taste the blood in my mouth.

'Right, back on the pitch, lads.' I can tell it's the master shouting. He leans over me and points to the big house, his hands waving and chopping the air.

'That's you for today, Donal. You can have a rest in the kitchen.'

He blows his whistle and runs on to the park again. The boys follow him. I'm left with the man with the black car who takes off his coat – it's sheepskin – and puts it over my shoulders.

'Are you OK to walk, son?'

'I am.'

I still feel like I'm underwater, but my head and my eye don't hurt any more – they're only numb.

In the kitchen the man sets me down on the green rug next to the range. He tells me to get a heat in my bones as he lights a cigarette from the hot coals.

I wait for the man to go back to the football game, to the master and the other boys, but he stays by the range, smoking his cigarette. He asks me do I want a puff, but I think he's trying to catch me out, and I don't want the switch again so I say no.

'I'm your friend, you know,' he says, kneeling down beside me.

I can smell the burning tobacco as he takes the coat off my shoulders and folds it over. 'Go on, lie down on that,' he says.

I'm staring into the grate where the hot coals are burning, and I see the orange sparks flying as he flicks his cigarette into the grate.

I hear the slapping noise of leather, the rattle of a brass buckle and the quick swish of my shorts being yanked down. I try to turn round, but I have a heavy hand pressed into my shoulders, forcing me into the green rug.

I can't move my top half; my legs go all over the place and my hips wriggle free of the rug, but suddenly I stop still and scream out. I've never felt pain like it. I look up at the burning coals and wonder has one of them just shot into me? It hurts more if I move at all, so I hold still, trying not to stray one inch.

The pain is all I know of agony for a few more seconds and then it's over. There's a new pain now, and it feels like a burning and jabbing in my belly.

I'm sobbing into the green rug. The sheepskin coat is torn away from me as the man goes to the door. He walks with his heels thumping on the hard hall floor, another door closes and then I hear the sound of an engine starting, and I know the man has gone back to the black car.

25

DI Bob Valentine watched Garry Keirns being led from the police saloon car in the parking bay. He was cuffed, as instructed, but didn't seem to be at all intimidated, striding forcefully beside the officers on his way into King Street station. A little while earlier, Freddie Gowan had been led in through the same doors; Jim Prentice would be taking Gowan's details right now, under instruction to go slow. So far, at least, Valentine's instructions were going to plan.

The knock on the glass door was timid and certainly didn't match CS Martin's usual style of arrival.

'Got a minute, Bob?' she said, peering beyond the jamb.

'Yes, of course. Come in.'

The CS closed the door behind her and walked towards Valentine at the window.

'Who's that?'

'Garry Keirns. Small-time local scrote from Cumnock who I'm sure knows more about these murders than he's letting on.'

'He looks like he's ready for the rack.'

'He's a very cocky lad, and he has some pretty heavy-weight backers.'

Martin turned away from the window. There were two

black PVC chairs in front of her. She sat down and indicated the empty one. 'I've been over the case files with Phil and Ally. They seem confident, verging on energised, if that's the right word.'

Valentine lowered himself into the chair; the cushion wheezed beneath him. 'They're not all corrupt bastards on my team.'

The chief super placed her hands in her lap and frowned. 'I spoke to the chief constable again. We both realise that we owe you an apology.'

'I take it you mentioned my request to transfer to the chief?'

'He was as shocked as I was – possibly even more so.'

The DI checked himself – his conscience was pressing. 'I was a little full on when we spoke earlier. Can I return the apology?'

'I'm glad you've calmed down now, Bob.' Martin fixed her gaze on the detective. 'Look, I understand what you're going through. I know you think I'm a bloody pen-pusher, but I see the challenges you're facing here. It can't be easy. I mean the case itself is bad enough without it being from the town you grew up in . . . And I heard about the funeral.'

'That's the least of my worries now. My old man knew Sandy a long time ago.'

'If you'd like to take some time, Bob, the chief constable can bring somebody else in.'

'No. That's not what I want.'

'Neither of us support a transfer – it's a non-starter. You're too valuable to the squad, and there's nobody ready to take over.'

'DS McCormack's ready.'

'Jesus, Bob, she's only come on board. How would Phil and Ally and the others respond to that?'

'They're police officers – they're used to having their noses put out of joint. And anyway, since when were the delicate feelings of the troops a consideration of the top brass? If that was the case Jim Prentice would have had his own squad by now.'

The chief super raised her hands in a gesture of resignation. She rose from her seat and headed for the door. Her temperament seemed to have altered as she turned and spoke to Valentine. The confidence was back in her voice. 'We've decided not to proceed with the public-relations secondment.'

'You both seemed pretty sure of this Stubbs woman the last time we spoke.'

'Priorities change, Bob.'

'Indeed they do.'

She closed the door firmly behind her.

As he tried to digest the conversation he'd just had with Martin, the detective found himself questioning his earlier judgement. Had he acted out of anger? That was never a good position to make a decision from. Had he been too close to his feelings for Clare and the girls when he requested a transfer? He didn't know. What he did know was that the about-turn by the chiefs had restored some of his pride, and that alone was enough to bolster some of his worth as a police officer.

The sudden confusion wouldn't help, and he knew that Martin was smart enough, or cunning enough, to play to his emotions. With Chief Constable Greaves backing her, she would feel confident enough of getting her own way, but Valentine knew the final word would be his – even if it meant quitting the force and walking away with nothing. He packed his thoughts on the transfer away – he could return to them when the case was no longer his main priority. Right now he had the interrogation of Garry Keirns to think about and just how Freddie Gowan would react to being pulled into the station.

The DI returned to the incident room and stood before the notes and photographs covering the whiteboard. The case was in a state of confusion – much of what they had was no more than a muddle of disparate facts. There was no common element, no core of related data to draw upon. He wondered if the task was beyond him – did the length of time that had elapsed since the crime had occurred make a solution impossible?

Valentine dipped his head before the board and started rubbing the back of his neck. Tension was creeping in now, along with doubt, and neither were welcome. He snapped upright, checked around the room to see if his look of defeat had been recorded but all eyes were down – he had got away with it this time, but he knew his doubts would need to be fended off with more resolve in future.

Someone had left a sandwich from the Tesco Express on his desk. There had once been some kind of ham salad between the slabs of brown bread, but now it was withered and shrunken; he was glad he had no appetite as he slid the offering towards the waste bin to clear the way for the case files. Valentine didn't know how long he had stared at the files, hoping for some illumination to come from the pages, but he did know when it was time to concede his efforts were proving fruitless.

On his way towards the interview rooms Valentine peered in the small reinforced-glass windows and noted where his interviewees were situated. Both Keirns and Gowan appeared agitated, stalking the confines of their small spaces and showing all the signs of impatience and indignation the DI would expect.

'Good,' said Valentine, under his breath. 'The edgier the better.'

He spotted DS McCormack and DS Donnelly waiting for him at the far end of the corridor. They were standing chatting between the custody sergeant's desk and a mop and bucket that was propped against the wall.

'How did it go?' said the DI to the detectives.

'Oh, hello, boss,' said McCormack. 'Gowan came quietly, no real fuss at all. There was some shock when he saw the red and white, though. I don't think it had really registered with him how serious matters were before then.'

'You were probably too polite. I should have sent Ally – he'd know how to noise him up.'

The officers laughed. 'Oh, he would that,' said Phil.

'And what about Keirns?' said Valentine.

'Huffed and puffed a bit, if truth be told,' said Donnelly.

'Before or after you cuffed him?'

'Both. Though there was a monumental kick-off when the cuffs went on. You know, he thinks he's bulletproof for some reason.'

'He might think that, Phil. But rest assured he'll soon be dispossessed of that notion . . . Did Keirns and Gowan see each other on the way in?'

'Yes indeed. Booked them in one after the other. It was a bit like that scene in *The Good, The Bad and The Ugly*. You know the one, when Clint's watching the spurs at the door and the ugly one comes in through the window.'

Valentine grinned. He was content that, so far anyway, things had gone to plan. 'I hope Garry Keirns got the surprise of his life.'

'To be honest, sir, I couldn't tell whether he was surprised, stunned or just bloody furious. He's a chancy customer, that one.'

'All the more reason to be careful. We need to keep our wits about us because if Keirns senses any weakness, he'll exploit it.'

'Like a rat in a maze, he's too dumb to know he's in a maze but just smart enough to sniff his way out, given half a chance.'

'Then we don't give him the chance,' said the DI. 'Right, let's go to work. Phil, you and Sylvia can get the rundown on the farm purchase from Gowan. I want any statement signed and sworn and admissible in court, so explain the laws of perjury very clearly to him. When DS McAlister appears, we'll make a start on the rat.'

26

Garry Keirns sat with his arms stretched out in front of him, his fingers drumming on the tabletop. When DI Bob Valentine and DS McAlister entered the interview room Keirns started to raise his hands, rubbing his wrists in animated fashion.

'I should be doing you for police brutality,' he bleated.

'Shut it, Garry. I'm in no mood to listen to any more of your pissing and whining.'

Keirns's features slumped into his face like he had been hit by a sudden gale. The fingers on his hands balled into fists and sunk beneath the line of the table. He was staring at the melamine surface when the DI slapped down a piece of white A4 paper composed of dense, closely typed words. 'Read it,' said Valentine.

Keirns eased himself forward and perched over the paper; he read only a few lines before sinking back in his chair.

'I've read it before.'

'Oh, you recognise your glowing reference, do you? I didn't.'

'What do you mean by that?'

'I mean what I say, Garry. I might have thought you'd

written it for yourself if I didn't know you struggled with joined-up writing, never mind typing.'

He shook his head. 'It's a genuine reference, I can assure you of that.'

'I'm sure it is. A genuine reference on genuine headed notepaper, by a genuine Member of Parliament. The only thing that's not genuine is the substance. I know you, Garry, and you're a dodgy wee scrote – nothing like the pillar of the community described in this letter.' Valentine snatched back the paper and proceeded to roam the room, reading and grinning to himself.

Keirns sat silently, breathing slowly through his gaping mouth.

'Nothing to say for yourself, Garry?'

'Like what?'

'Like how you came by the support of an MP? And remember I've seen your rap sheet.'

'What does it matter, the MP's dead now.'

'I know Andy Lucas is dead. I checked the guy out, or should say I'm still in the process of checking him out, but what I have found out makes for some interesting reading.'

Keirns stooped in his chair and faced the DI. He seemed to be fighting off an accusation that he'd imagined himself. 'I ran respectable community groups – I was praised for my work by many people. You can't try and blacken my name just because it suits you, Detective.'

'Yes, you ran boys' groups, football, cricket, that kind of thing. But, Garry, who said anything about blackening your name?'

'That's what's coming.' He folded his arms and sat stiffly, as if waiting for more serious confrontation. 'I can feel it.'

Valentine returned to the table and removed a chair for himself. When he sat down, his voice had softened. 'Are you referring to the rumours about Andy Lucas after he died?'

'I don't listen to tittle-tattle.'

'But you must have read the papers when they were full of that Columba House business. There were four men convicted on sex offences against twenty-nine Columba boys.'

'All rubbish.'

'One of the rapists was the school's master, Garry. You must have known the man.'

'What are you trying to say?'

'They jailed those men, Garry. And they closed the school.'

'I know that. It was my school too, but I'd left the place years earlier.'

'Six years earlier. But you didn't go far, did you?'

'I went to the farm. You know that.'

Valentine eased back in his chair. He was enjoying watching the pressure mounting on Keirns. 'I know lots of things, Garry. Some of them I hear from people, though, and I just don't know if they're telling me the truth.'

Keirns's eyes flared. 'What are you on about?'

'I hear your MP friend committed suicide, about the time of the Columba House trials. I hear that some folk thought he was going to be added to the list of child rapists.'

'I don't know anything about that.'

'Do you know what I think, Garry? I think you remember what you want to remember and discard the rest. I think you should be a little less selective and a hell of a lot more honest, because you don't have any friends in high places looking after you now. Andy Lucas is dead – who was looking out for him?'

Valentine got up from the table and walked towards the door of the interview room, followed by DS McAlister. A uniformed officer opened the door to let them out. No one looked back at Garry Keirns as they left.

In the corridor McAlister spoke. 'Well that's put the shits up him, boss.'

'Somebody has to. He's holding out on us.'

'It's beginning to look obvious, but he might not look so scared if he knew how little we had to go on.'

'We'll get there.' Valentine checked in the interview room across the hall. McCormack and Donnelly were bringing proceedings to a close. As they left, closing the door behind them, Valentine was the first to address them. 'Well?'

'He coughed, sir,' said Donnelly.

'For what?'

'He admitted the deal with Keirns was signed two years ago, quite a while before Sandy Thompson passed away.'

'Did Keirns even have authority to sell the property back then?'

McCormack answered the question. 'Gowan's adamant that he did. Blairgowan has documentation showing the deeds were in Keirns's name when the contract was signed.'

'So Garry Keirns managed to get his mitts on Sandy's place before he'd even died. I know for a fact that Sandy wasn't *compos mentis* in the years before he died so there must have been some coercion.'

'Or blackmail,' said Donnelly.

'The problem will be proving it,' said McCormack.

'There's no way of proving it – Sandy's dead. But if Keirns was so worried about how it looked selling to Blairgowan whilst he was alive then he must have something to hide.'

'Like what, sir?' said McAlister. 'I'm not convinced Keirns cares that much what people think of him.'

'Oh, he cares. But only what *certain* people think, Ally. If he held off on the Blairgowan deal until Sandy died, it was because someone didn't like the way it might look and told him so.'

27

'Let Freddie Gowan go,' said Valentine. The team watched the DI. Clearly they'd absorbed the information, but they didn't move.

'And what about Keirns, boss?' said McAlister.

'We can hold him for twenty-four hours without charge, and that's what I intend to do.'

'And after that?'

'A lot can happen in twenty-four hours, Ally. I want to see how he reacts to this new revelation from Gowan about the sale of Ardinsh Farm, but I want him to fester on our little chat before I put that to him.'

'Yes, sir,' said McAlister. The team still hadn't moved.

'Right, give Gowan his marching orders, then I'll see you all upstairs for a briefing in the incident room.'

DS McCormack proceeded to the custody sergeant's desk, and the others followed Valentine on to the stairs.

'What's your thinking on all of this now, sir?' said Donnelly.

'I'm trying not to think. It's all such a bloody hotchpotch at the moment I'd only be reacting. We need more to go on, but let's say Garry Keirns just went from a person of interest to a suspect.'

McAlister and Donnelly exchanged glances. Their expressions were moving towards doubt but neither spoke up.

'Sir, we've nothing solid to charge him with,' said McAlister.

Valentine halted mid-stride. 'Do you think I don't know that?'

'But you just said . . .'

'Ally, I can still suspect the wee scrote without having the goods on him. With any luck that'll come.' He resumed his path on the stairwell; they were nearing their floor. 'Get your files together. When Sylvia shows we'll gather at the board.'

'Yes, sir.'

Valentine paced through to his office. He was moving with greater purpose, with a sense that time was pressing. At his computer terminal he checked his email for the site picture from Mike Sullivan, but nothing had appeared. He picked up the phone.

'Mike, it's Bob . . .'

'Bernie's just in the door. I'm scanning the shot as we speak.'

'Great. How's it looking?'

'Bob, it's better than I thought. You won't get a solid ID out of it, but there's distinguishing marks that could sway a jury.'

'Tell me more.'

'You'll see for yourself.' Sullivan seemed eager to change the subject – he was racing his words out. 'There's more too, and you'll like this even better.'

'I think I like it already. Go on . . .'

Sullivan coughed away from the phone. 'Do you

remember the list we gave you for the contents we retrieved from the barrel?'

'The catalogued evidence file, yes, I have it here some-where.' Valentine moved papers around on his desk then opened his drawer – the catalogue was sitting on the top. 'Right, I have it in front of me.'

'OK, it's Item Twelve I want to draw your attention to.'

Valentine ran his finger down the index. 'The bookie's pen. Small red one.'

'That's it.'

'Well, what about it?'

'That was found in one of the boys' pockets, the older one. It's a stretch, but if we can tie in the batch numbers then we have a definite link to the boys and the farmhouse.'

'You found another bookie's pen?'

'Bob, we found a bag of them. Must be about fifty in there. They were stuffed away under the boards.'

'Print them, Mike. And run anything you find alongside Garry Keirns's prints that we have on record. If we can establish a link, we might have the bastard.'

Valentine put down the telephone and calmly tapped his thumbnail on the back of his lips. It was a pose he often adopted when he was in deep thought. For a moment, he wondered about running through to tell the squad, but his mind drifted into a higher place.

As he closed his eyes, Valentine saw Rory Stevenson with another boy. They were in a Cumnock street playing football. At either side of the road the boys lobbed the ball towards each other until one struck the kerb and the ball bounced back over the road.

The boys yelled out, but Valentine couldn't hear their

words – everything was muffled. The light started to take on a strange quality, and soon he seemed to be viewing the boys down a telescope. They walked away, one with the ball under his arm and the other showing him something small that he'd removed from his pocket.

They talked excitedly, but their words were a mystery to Valentine. Only the sight of the little penknife being admired by Rory seemed to speak to him. It was the knife the DI had seen on the list of evidence reclaimed from the barrel.

Valentine opened his eyes and reached for the list, scanning the index once again. It was there – two places below the bookie's pen was a penknife with the same bookie's name on it: Carson's.

The PC pinged, alerting Valentine to the incoming email. He opened up the picture right away and stared at the screen. He couldn't properly absorb what he was seeing. The shot was contorted, positioned at an unnatural angle, but there was enough to make out the prominent features. He clicked on print to send the file to the colour printer in the incident room.

On his way out the door Valentine rallied the team. 'Right, Sylvia, you're back. Can I have the rest of you round the board directly please?'

There was the immediate sound of castors scraping on the floor, accompanied by a murmur of low voices as the squad gravitated towards the middle of the room. When Valentine retrieved the photographic print he held it away from himself to better view the whole picture. It was worse than he imagined.

'Right, Sylvia, what's the SP on this Blairgowan mob?' said the DI.

DS McCormack approached the front of the small gathering and crossed her arms. She leaned against the wall as she began to speak. 'The man who has been of most interest to us is Freddie Gowan so far. I'll come to his partner Pete Blair in a moment.'

'Have you pulled records, Sylvia?' said Valentine.

'Yes, boss. Both clear. Gowan is a pretty heavy-footed driver but then, well, you've seen his motor.'

The group emitted a low titter.

DS McCormack continued, 'Gowan's Glasgow born and bred, and as far as I can ascertain – and I think I've been very rigorous – this is his first job in Ayrshire, certainly his first major project here under Blairgowan.'

'And the other bloke?' said Valentine.

'Yes, Pete Blair's an interesting character. He's basically an accountant, made a lot of money by the looks of things and likes to spread it around. He's a silent partner though, so isn't actively involved in the day-to-day running, which he leaves to Gowan.'

'What other lines is he in?'

'You name it, really. He's got a chain of pound stores and substantial interests in more than a few golf courses. But again no Ayrshire connections. I don't think he's even visited the site in Cumnock.'

'I'm finding it hard to see them in the frame,' said DS Donnelly.

'Me too, Phil,' said McCormack. 'And that's where I am with it. They're both legit, and Blairgowan's a profitable business with its taxes all up to date. In this day and age, that's a rarity surely.'

Valentine approached the board, holding the photograph

to his chest. 'I won't change my initial opinion of Freddie Gowan,' he said. 'I still think he's a cowboy, but if we banged up every builder that was overambitious who'd have put my new kitchen in?'

Abrupt laughter burst through the gathering. 'Right, and to change the mood entirely,' said Valentine, pinning up the new photograph, 'take a very close look at this, and my apologies for the bluntness of the content.'

'God, do we have to look?' said McCormack.

'I'm sorry,' said Valentine. 'But I'm afraid this is what we're dealing with. Please take a moment to think about the kind of beast we're after.'

28

The photograph that Valentine had pinned on the white-board was positioned higher than the other scenes of crime shots. It loomed over the pathology pictures of the mummified corpses of the boys and was higher than the horrific first find of the open barrel.

The murder squad stared in reverent silence, at first seeming to ascertain whether the child in the picture was one of the victims. The man, who was positioned most prominently in the scene, was headless though his appearance gave odd hints to his identification.

The child was merely a boy, perhaps ten years old at the most. His face, contorted in pain, sat beneath a blond fringe, cut in a straight line. It was the kind of haircut Valentine recalled all the boys having from those days – a pudding-basin cut – and the sight of it disturbed old memories.

The man, who seemed tall even without his head, was in office attire. Blue pinstripe trousers, slackened at the waist, and a paler blue shirt with open white collars, a red paisley-print tie looped round his neck. His right hand, thrust forward and gripping the boy's thin shoulder displayed a gold signet ring on the smallest finger. The picture would have been disturbing enough with only the boy's agony showing on his face, but the confirmation of an adult engaged in rape made the image even more harrowing.

'Can we take that down now?' said DS McCormack.

Valentine nodded. 'If you've all seen it.'

Heads nodded around the table. The temperature of the room seemed to have dropped.

'As I said, I'm sorry to have to show you that,' said Valentine.

'Where did we get this?' said McAlister.

'Bernie's team found it under the floorboards at Ardinsh. It's just in, along with a bag of about fifty bookie's pens matching the one we retrieved from the oil drum.'

McAlister snatched his words. 'Well, you know what they were bloody well for!'

'Bribing kids is my best bet,' said Valentine.

'Paedo bastards,' said McAlister. He shook his head and returned the DI's gaze.

'OK, Ally, settle down. I know this is hard for everyone – these cases are always emotional – but we need to remain rational and logical if we're to get a result here.'

DS Donnelly had turned over the picture again. 'This ring's got markings on it.'

'I saw that,' said Valentine.

'I think we can get the boffins to blow that up.'

'We'll give it a go. I've asked for prints on the bookie's pens. With any luck we've got Keirns's dabs all over them. Which reminds me – he's still downstairs. Can someone request a thirty-two-hour custody extension in light of this new evidence?'

DS McCormack nodded. 'I'll get on that with the chief super, sir.'

'Thanks, Sylvia. I don't think you'll have any bother, Dino's still tiptoeing around us,' said Valentine. 'Who's up next then? *Phil*, what can you tell us about your dealings with Columba House?'

DS Donnelly strolled towards the board, dropping a blue folder on the tabletop.

'To say this has been a nightmare would be the understatement of the century. Columba House is, as you know, no more. They ceased to be in 1989 after four convictions were upheld against the staff, including the master, Trevor Healey, and involving twenty-nine boys.'

'Try and keep to the bare details, Phil. We've still to hear from Ally, and we're on the clock, remember,' said Valentine.

'Yes, boss,' said Donnelly. 'All the press cuttings are there on the case if you want to delve into them for yourself, and I believe there's still some with Colleen if you're super keen. I've been through the lot and it makes grim reading, I can assure you. However there were one or two interesting snippets of information that I pulled out.'

'What's that then?' said McAlister.

'I'm just coming to it. Right, bear with me because it gets complicated. The initial investigator on the case was a bloke called Den Rennie from Glasgow CID. He was replaced by an assistant chief constable no less called Eric Pollock, now Sir Eric Pollock.'

Valentine interrupted. 'Wait a minute, why was Rennie replaced?'

'Good question, and one I've asked myself, but the closest I can come to an answer is he fell foul of the press.'

'In what way?'

'There was some kind of a stoush. I never got to the bottom of it, but it ended up with Rennie either being told to clamp it or choosing to avoid the press altogether.'

'That would have gone down well with a case this sensitive.'

'You better believe it. I'll come back to Rennie in a minute. So Pollock's parachuted in from the capital, and he wraps up the investigation in a matter of weeks.'

'Convenient,' said McAlister.

'It gets better. Then Pollock promptly retires. The Columba House investigation was his last case. Now he lives in Spain and has a knighthood for services to the police force.'

Valentine put his hand in his pocket; he felt the St Christopher there. 'And what became of Den Rennie?'

'He went back to Glasgow CID I suppose.'

'No, you said there was more on him.'

Donnelly pointed to the ceiling and snapped his fingers. 'That's right. Forgetting myself. Rennie did eventually break his silence with the press when the MP Andy Lucas committed suicide, and guess what he said?'

'Don't tell me he doubted it was a suicide?' blurted Valentine.

'Got it in one. But that was his final utterance in print.'

'How far have you got with the Columba House people on this?' said Valentine.

'Not far at all. They're officially defunct, as you know, and the umbrella organisation, the charity group they were part of, consists of an answering machine. The one time I did get a reply they directed me to a group of lawyers, who directed me to a PR firm that said Columba House is no longer a client of theirs. There's no files held, no records, no data. The story is they were liquidated, but in reality it's like they never existed.'

'OK, Phil, good work. It might not have led us anywhere, but I appreciate the yards you've put in,' said Valentine. 'Your next job is to get hold of Den Rennie, and I want it done on the QT, if you know what I mean.'

'An off-the-record chat, sir?'

'Well, given there's bugger all written down on any of this then it would be pointless putting it on record.' Valentine signalled to DS McAlister to indicate he was moving on. 'Right, Ally, you're up next.'

'Well, I had the grim task of going over the cold-case files, as you know,' said McAlister.

'Nice wee break, was it?' said Donnelly.

'That'll be right, Phil. Now, as I was saying, our favoured cold case involved two missing boys, Donal Welsh, who was eleven, and Rory Stevenson, aged ten. Donal, according to the files, was a Columba House boy, and Rory was the only son of an ex-miner from Cumnock who ran a bike-repair shop at the time.'

'Seems a strange pair to get together,' said DS McCormack.

'Yeah, the Columba boys were pariahs – they didn't mix with the lads from the town,' said Valentine.

'The case files highlight that too, sir. But there's a lot of speculation from DI John Corrigan and not a lot you'd call concrete.'

'They certainly didn't have what we have, Ally.'

'That's for sure, sir.' McAlister opened one of the files on top of the table and picked up a press cutting. 'The boys went missing quite a while before the Columba House case too. This was 1984 that they were reported missing, and there's no mention of abuse allegations in the case files – nothing linking the two investigations at all.'

'What were the investigating officer's conclusions?' said Valentine.

'Corrigan's a bit vague on that. He takes a lot of stabs in the dark, but it's clear the case was going nowhere.'

'He must have had some kind of guess.'

'He seems to edge towards a serial killer snatching, sir. We know there were a number operational in the area, or near to the district, that we learnt about later so it's not the wildest assumption.'

'And Corrigan, where is he now?'

'Retired, sir. His file says he lives in Prestwick. I was planning to pay him a visit as soon as possible.'

'Do that, Ally. And have the highlights of these files copied for all senior officers too.'

'Will do.'

'Now, this ex-miner with the bike shop?' said the DI.

McAlister replaced the file on top of the pile and turned back to face the group. 'Yes, Colin Stevenson. He's still married to Rory's mother, Marie, and they both live in the same council house in Cumnock. He was their only child. I can't imagine how hard the grief has hit them over the years.'

'It must have been painful,' said Valentine. 'And it's about to get more painful. We'll have to pay them a visit and ask them to take a look at what we think are some of Rory's personal effects.'

'Yes, boss. They won't be able to identify him from his remains, that's for sure.'

29

On the way down the stairwell the view passing the window was of grey and weary buildings. A thin line of roof stacks slanted towards the pink horizon in a rugged rut. The evening outside the station was of perfect stillness, pierced only with the hum of traffic and eerie noises of playing children. As he descended, thinking about the visit he must make to Rory Stevenson's parents later, Valentine felt his thoughts swaying inside him. He didn't want to hear the children's voices – he wanted to block them out, and that wounded him because no matter how much he hated in the world, he knew there was always much to love too.

'How do you want to play this, boss?' said DS McAlister. His words were followed by the roar of a motorcycle outside.

Valentine turned. 'What are you talking about – the visit to the parents or our next meeting with Keirns?'

'To be honest, I'm trying not to think about the visit to Cumnock.'

Valentine continued down the stairs. 'That's probably best, Ally. Leave that to me. As for Keirns, we're going straight for the jugular. I aim to put the fear of God into him, and failing that I'll settle for the fear of being banged up on a double murder charge.'

The sounds of heavy heels clacking on the hard flooring echoed with them down the stairwell. At the interview suite the officers approached the desk sergeant and waited for Keirns to be brought through again.

'How did his partner in crime depart earlier?' said Valentine.

'Are you on about Freddie Gowan?' said the officer.

'The very man.'

'He was a bit sheepish, didn't say much, which was in stark contrast to how he arrived.'

The DI was pleased with the sergeant's assessment; he only hoped that by hauling them both in together that the same might be true for Keirns.

When he showed up from the custody cells, Keirns was staring at the floor. He glanced upwards at the detectives but chose not to respond. His mood was unreadable – he might have been bristling with anger or succumbing to weary acceptance.

As the detectives entered the room, Valentine eyed Keirns closely. Skin was sitting in folds beneath his eyes – was it a sign of fatigue? The DI hoped so as he stood before Keirns, rolling up his shirtsleeves. He let the suspect take in the full importance of the occasion before leaning over the desk and smiling.

'Looks like you have some explaining to do, Garry.' Valentine slapped down a blue folder.

'What?' said Keirns.

'Did you miss me whilst I was away?'

'*What?*'

171

'I said did you miss me? You know, the old Bob Valentine, the one that sat you down in this very interview room and spoke nicely to you about my horrific current workload. If you didn't miss him, you should now. Because, Garry, the one standing before you is bringing some life-shattering news.'

'Stop playing games with me, Valentine.'

The DI let his smile fade and removed the chair. He sat down opposite the suspect. 'Do you like the ponies, Garry?'

'As much as the next man.'

'Oh, I bet you like them more than the once-a-year Grand National punter.'

'What's this got to do with anything?'

'Go to the Gold Cup every year, I bet.'

'Maybe.'

'Like to put a regular line on . . . My old man used to like the bookies – it's a Cumnock thing.'

'So what?'

A block of bright sunlight divided the room into light and shade. Valentine loosened off his tie and opened the top button of his shirt. 'Yeah, he used to put a line on every Saturday. Went to a place on the main street called Carson's. Do you know it?'

Keirns shrugged. He looked through Valentine with a tense and hesitant gaze.

'When I was a boy, quite a few years ago now, my dad used to bring me home those wee bookie's pens from there. The red ones. I loved them.'

Keirns's skin grew waxy. He touched his hands together then moved them like he was lathering soap.

'I see you remember those wee Carson's pens too, Garry.'

'What if I do? It isn't a crime, is it?'

'No, it's no crime.' Valentine reached out for the folder and opened it. He let a few seconds pass before he turned over the first page and proceeded to read.

'That's forty-three bagged up and a further five loose, so that makes forty-eight little red bookie's pens in total . . . retrieved from your old home this very day.'

Keirns looked smaller before the detective, sitting hunched up and shrunken in the chair. 'You searched the farm. Why would you do that?'

'I'm asking the questions, Garry, if you don't mind. You see that's how we do these things. That's how we investigate the murders of little boys. That is, Garry, how we interrogate murder suspects.'

Keirns's head jerked. 'I didn't kill them.'

Valentine wasn't listening. 'Did you hear that total? Forty-eight little bookie's pens tucked away under the floorboards.' He sat back and put his hands behind his head as he called out to DS McAlister. 'Why would any grown man have so many pens hidden away like that, Ally?'

DS McAlister approached the table and perched himself on the edge beside the DI. He stared directly at Keirns as he spoke. 'No good reason I can think of, boss.'

'I once knew a suspect who kept a great big tub of lollipops under his bed . . . but he was a paedophile.'

'A beast?' said McAlister.

'Yes, Ally, I believe that's what they call them inside. Our lollipop man is in Peterhead now, by the way. Having a terrible time of it too. He was stabbed with a chicken bone and beaten to a pulp a couple of times.'

173

'They don't like beasts inside, boss.'

The conversation was interrupted. 'I didn't do it!' Keirns lunged forward, banging his hands on the table. His chair fell down behind him, crashing loudly on the hard surface.

McAlister grabbed Keirns by the shoulders and yanked him away from the DI. He pressed Keirns into the corner and pinned him there whilst he roared above the suspect's rantings. When Keirns quietened McAlister stepped away and retrieved the chair from the ground.

'Get back here now, Garry,' said Valentine.

Keirns retraced his steps. His breathing grew more stertorous with every pace. When he sat down he was sweating. He gripped his arms around his stomach like he was suffering cramps.

'Now, Garry, I think we both know what those bookie's pens were for because there was one in the barrel with those poor wee boys we found murdered on your old farm.'

'I never touched those boys.'

'Oh, come on, Garry. Do you expect us to believe that? I said we found one of your pens with the victims.'

'It could have come from anywhere – you said so yourself that you had them.'

'Ah but, Garry, I haven't had two wee lads murdered in my back garden. That's what you call creating an element of doubt. The courts are big on that kind of thing.'

'Right, that's it. I want to get a solicitor now. I'm telling you I want a solicitor, do you hear me?'

Valentine cleared his face of all expression and reached out once again for the folder on the table. As he drew it to him he spoke softly. 'Your response to the pens has been duly noted, Garry. I'd now like to get your impression of another

174

item we found secreted in a manila envelope, beneath the floorboards of the property you arranged to sell to Freddie Gowan two years before Sandy Thompson died.'

Keirns was following the DI's words as if he was lip-reading. He seemed almost unaware that the photograph of the headless man had been presented to him. When he looked down, towards the table and the photograph, he fell silent. The image didn't seem to create the confusion it had done for everyone else. There was no head twisting, eye shifting or balancing of the abstruse elements of the picture. Keirns pushed the item away.

'Well?' said Valentine.

There was no reply.

'Do you know the man in this picture, Garry?'

Keirns looked towards the wall. 'Put it away.'

'A yes or a no would do, Garry.'

The suspect continued to stare at the wall but refused to speak any more. There was a brief, repeated demand for a solicitor, which the officers rebuffed. When it became clear Keirns had given his final words, the DI and DS collected their files and left the suspect alone.

Outside the interview room Valentine halted to address McAlister in the corridor.

'Well?' he said.

'He's shitting it, boss.'

'He knows we're on to him.'

'Did you see the way he looked at that picture?'

'Yes, like he'd seen it before. Nobody else could make hide nor hair of it.'

McAlister's eyes remained on the pacing DI. 'So what now? We can't charge him unless he coughs.'

'No, we don't have nearly enough to charge him. We need to keep the pressure on though. He knows we're close to finding answers, I could sense it on him. Jesus Christ, I can feel it myself.'

'Do we get him a solicitor, sir?'

'No, we let him go.'

'But we've got thirty-two hours. Sylvia got the extension.'

'Let him go now. I'm more interested to see what he does under the influence of panic.'

McAlister's face tightened, the features sharpening as he turned back to the interview room. 'Are you sure about this, boss?'

'Yes, Ally. Let Keirns walk. But not before you have two officers at his backside 24-7.'

30

February 1984

It's getting harder to remember what Mammy's face looked like. Sometimes, when I close my eyes and really concentrate, I think I can see her smiling, but I'm not sure. I used to say, to myself only, that she was always smiling, that was how I remembered her, but I don't know so much now. It seems a long time ago, like in the fairy stories they tell you. Maybe that's it, maybe I read about her somewhere or someone told me and that's what happened. She was a princess who died, and I was just wishing she'd come back to life. She never did though. I'll never believe those stories again – all those happy endings are just stuff and nonsense.

The car bumps over the road and the new boys laugh and joke about it. They have pop, that's what the man with pig eyes calls it. He's English – I know the accent because the boys say he's posh.

'Come on, Donal, drink some pop!' says one of the boys. I take a sip and he says get it down you, and the man with the pig eyes agrees, so I slug a good whack of it.

'Aren't you mad excited?' says the boy.

'I suppose,' I say, and that just makes him grin wider.

There's four of us – five if you include Terry, who sits in the front beside the man with the pig eyes. Terry's his favourite, we can all tell. You can always tell when the men have a favourite because there's chocolate galore and lucky bags with the cola bottles inside that every boy likes. Sometimes – well, once – there were football stickers, but they made us hand them all back and even went through my pockets for them. I don't know why they'd have to do that. There's lots of things like that, though they say it's all part of the excitement.

'I love a party,' says Terry.

The man driving the car turns to him and smiles and says will we have a sing-song. I don't know the words – something about a young boy of sixteen summers. I don't like the singing much.

When we get there it's dark. The night sky is not quite black yet, and there's some blue still at the edges where there's also a white glow. The man with the pig eyes says we'll go in the back way and isn't that exciting too, but I don't answer him.

I remember the last place like this. It was a big hotel in the middle of nowhere. There were lots of boys I didn't know, all running around bare chested and with the bright red cheeks on them. All the grown-ups were men too, and they would let you try a fag on your own or give you beer if you asked. I didn't like them; they smiled too much.

Inside Terry gets a piggyback from the man who drove us, and there's lots of noise and boys running around all over the place. One boy is sick on the carpet and gets taken away, and I wonder if he's going to be put to bed early. There'll be lots of beds in lots of rooms – I know this from before.

'Would you like some more pop, young man?' says the man with the pig eyes. He's put down Terry now and has a tray with bottles of Coke on it. I take one and a straw, because I'm very thirsty. I don't remember ever being this thirsty before and then my cheeks feel very warm as well.

I wonder will I be sick like the other boy, and then the man with the pig eyes is pointing at me and I hear him saying my name. He brings over a man and says his name. I think it's Bunny. It doesn't sound like a man's name.

'Hello,' he says.

I don't answer.

'One of the quiet ones, are you?'

I shrug.

'That looks nice.' He nods at my drink. 'Is it nice?'

'Yes.'

'I bet I know what you like. Meringues, great big ones with cream and a cherry on top!'

I don't feel like eating. I drink some more Coke and everything starts to go funny, like I'm looking through a river to the stones below.

'No. Well maybe later you'll feel like it.' He bends down and his eyes are level with mine, but I can't look there. I look at the shoulder of his jacket, at the little white balls that are falling from his head. He smells of a scent I don't think I've ever smelt before but I know I'll always remember wherever I go.

'You look ready for a nap, come to Bunny.' He picks me up and says off we hop, and my face is on his shoulder with the little bits of white gritty balls. I want to move them, to push them away, but I'm too sleepy now.

'Bunny will tuck you in, young man.'

179

The walls are green with a pale white light shining from above. When he puts me on the bed I feel like I'm sinking, like the bed is swallowing me up. The man starts to lift my arms and pull my jumper over my head. I want to say no, leave me, but I can't talk either – it's like I'm frozen.

When all my clothes are on the floor and I lie on top of the bed naked, he starts to undress himself. He has a purple tie and he rolls it round his hand, all the time looking over me, up and down, up and down.

He says something that sounds like horns in my ears. It's words though, I know it. I want to cry out, to go home, but I feel trapped.

The man puts down his tie and undoes his shirt buttons, one by one. He has a flat, white chest with deep black patches of hair on his nipples. He watches me all the while, as he unbuckles his belt and lets his trousers fall, as he takes off his white underpants and climbs on the bed, stroking me with his long, thin fingers that roam all over me.

31

A blackbird was sitting on the roof of the car as Valentine and McAlister entered the station car park. It seemed settled, quite comfortable, then its yellow beak twitched and it darted off towards the dimming sky.

The DI handed the keys to McAlister. 'You can drive.'

'Sure. Any particular reason?'

'Because there usually is, you mean? Yes, Ally, after you've dropped me off at home you're heading out to Prestwick to take John Corrigan's pulse.'

'Right. I can do that.'

'Keep it light, chatty. I don't suppose he'll reveal anything more than we have from his files, but I don't want to leave any stones unturned.'

McAlister started the car and pulled away from the station. As they left the King Street roundabout the DI called on the radio for the address in Prestwick.

As they travelled Valentine ran his fingers through his hair, massaging his scalp. He had a deep tension building inside him that he couldn't account for. It wasn't the progress that they'd made on the case that worried him – it was something beyond that. He stopped rubbing his head and a few seconds later realised he was massaging his wrist in much the same manner.

As they headed to Masonhill a small, flat moon sat high above the clouds. Two hollows, either side of the moon, marked gaps in the covering of sky, adding to the unreality of the evening. Valentine reached into his pocket to touch the St Christopher pendant and pinched it between his fingertips. It was a reassuring act that he couldn't explain; as if in some way it signalled a kind of communication with the dead boy it had belonged to.

As McAlister halted the car outside the DI's home the passenger door opened. Valentine hung a leg from the car momentarily as he spoke. 'One hour, back here.'

'Yes, sir.'

Valentine hurried across the tarmac to his driveway and on through the front door of his house. As he removed his jacket his wife stuck her head round the kitchen door.

'Wonders will never cease,' she said mockingly. 'You're home for dinner twice in the space of a week.'

The DI approached her. She was holding a cooking pot with a wooden handle; a slew of pasta was being turned inside. 'Hello, love.'

'So you are home?' she said.

'Not quite. I'll grab a bite but I'm off again.'

Clare put down the pot. The hob hissed. 'Hang on. What is this?'

Valentine knew the look immediately. As his wife fastened her gaze on him, tight radial lines darted from the edges of her eyes.

'Clare, I've no time to explain just now.'

'You better try.'

'I've asked for a transfer.' The blurted response blind-sided his wife.

'You have?'

'With Martin and also the chief constable.'

'*Really?*'

'Yes, really.' He leaned forward and placed a kiss on his smiling wife's cheek. 'But we'll have to talk about it later. I'm not going anywhere until this case is solved. I feel close, Clare, really close.'

He headed for the living room, leaving his wife with a pinched expression on her face like she might start to whistle. He couldn't interpret the look, but it wasn't one he felt threatened by – they were much easier to decipher.

His father was the first to speak when Valentine opened the door, his daughters being too engrossed in *Hollyoaks*.

'Hello, son. You're early tonight.'

Valentine let his thoughts run. 'Remember that bookies on the main street, the old one, Carson's?'

'Oh, aye. It's gone now. Think it's a Gregg's, isn't it?'

'Did you know the bloke who owned it?'

'The bookie? It was big Alan Carson. I knew him a bit, to say hello to, like. He's buried up next to your mother.'

'Oh . . .'

His father leaned forward in his chair. A newspaper fell from his lap on to the floor. 'Why do you ask?'

'Just work, Dad.' Valentine rose. 'Did Sandy use that book-ies?'

'God no. Sandy didn't bet – he was far too tight.'

'What about Garry Keirns?'

'Oh he had a line on every other day. Never won a thing,

mind. He must have been big Alan's favourite customer. He was never the luckiest.'

'Well, his luck's just about run out now. Thanks, Dad.'

Valentine drifted through dinner. His thoughts played tag between the past and the present. He was stuck somewhere in the middle of the two, reminiscing about his childhood in one moment and revisiting the case the next. There was a gap, something he had missed, but he couldn't figure out what it was. He knew he didn't have all the pieces of the puzzle, but what he did possess was a newfound optimism.

When the doorbell rang Valentine shot from his seat at the dinner table. 'That'll be Ally,' he said. 'I'll have to love you and leave you.'

On the road to Cumnock DS McAlister started to detail the meeting he'd just had with the retired detective John Corrigan.

'He was broken up, you know,' said McAlister.

'In what way?'

'The investigation went nowhere and he knew it. He felt for the Stevensons – he got to know them quite well.'

'That's understandable.'

'Yeah. The other lad, though, no one mourned him.'

Valentine looked over to McAlister. He was gripping tight to the wheel. 'Not a soul questioned the investigation. He was missing for nearly three full days before Columba's master notified police.'

'Three bloody days?'

'Yes, sir. Corrigan said the boy was a ward of state, no parents to trace. But even still, you'd think someone would report him missing sooner than three days afterwards.'

'Was that all you found out?' said Valentine.

'The Columba boy, Donal Welsh – there was something else Corrigan found strange.'

'Go on.'

'He said Healey, the master, only reported him missing after the press reported that Rory Stevenson wasn't alone. There were multiple sightings, all of two boys.'

'Did Corrigan question Healey?'

'Oh, yeah, he did. Healey said he had been on leave for two days and blame shifted on to his lack of staff, lack of funding, lack of anyone giving a shit really.'

'And Corrigan bought that?'

'No. He didn't at all. At least that's what he said to me. Corrigan said he wasn't surprised in the slightest when Trevor Healey went down five years later as a child molester.'

'Isn't hindsight a great thing?' said the DI.

McAlister nodded. He flicked on the blinkers and turned the wheel. He was straightening the car as he glanced back towards the DI. 'I'm inclined to give Corrigan the benefit of the doubt, boss. He didn't have the evidence we have to go on.'

'Oh come on. You'll be telling me we didn't know how to take fingerprints in the eighties next.'

'He seemed genuinely moved when I told him about the mummified bodies in the barrel. He wants this bastard behind bars as much as us.'

The car drew to a halt. 'Is this it?'

'Elizabeth Crescent. That's the place there.'

'That looks like the parents coming over, sir.'

'They have names – Colin and Marie. They're real people, Ally, and I can think of no easy way to tell them that we reckon we've found the son they lost thirty-two years ago.'

32

It was Colin Stevenson that Valentine turned to first. He was a stolid-looking man, dressed sombrely in highly polished black shoes, dress trousers and a shirt, rolled up at the sleeves but buttoned at the collar, beneath a tightly knotted tie. With the swept-back hair and the easy manners he looked out of place in 2016 – he was more like a relic of 1955.

When Colin spoke, his voice was so low the DI had to strain his ears to hear him. The soft timbre didn't reveal anything, however – the man's emotions were cached away.

'I'm Detective Inspector Bob Valentine, and this is my colleague DS McAlister.'

'Shall we go inside, gentlemen?'

The officers followed behind. Marie required a supporting arm from her husband, her thin shoulders trembling beneath the light navy cardigan she had wrapped around her. She sniffed into a white handkerchief as she went, each breathy exhalation clogged with emotion.

The house in Elizabeth Crescent was smaller than it looked from the outside, but by today's standard of council property the interior was roomy. The walls were covered with naive watercolours, Ayrshire scenes mainly – Greenan Castle, the Isle of Arran seen from the coast and a ramshackle Burns Cottage. Occasionally the face of a small boy was recognisable to Valentine. In happier conditions the DI would have remarked upon the pictures, inquired after the artist, but it didn't seem appropriate. He thought he might never know which of the two parents had wiled away the tortuous hours in the distraction of paint and brushes.

'Can I get you anything, some tea?' said Colin.

'We're fine thanks.'

The man seemed wounded by the rejection of his offer, his eyelids double blinking to reveal a dull gaze. It was the first hint of unease he had displayed and belied his stiff appearance.

'Mr and Mrs Stevenson, we're here with some news about your boy, Rory,' said Valentine.

The couple clung to each other on the sofa, the sharp knuckles showing the tightness of the grip. 'Have you found him, Detective?' said Colin.

As Valentine tried to answer the question he became dimly aware of another figure standing in the doorway. He felt a shiver pass through his jowls and his mouth dried over. Speech was prevented as he stared at the small frame in grey.

'Detective?' said Colin.

Valentine's face sat slack above his neck. He tried to turn but found he couldn't. Rory Stevenson stood splay-footed before him. There was a football under his arm, which he started to bounce on the floor. The vibration shook the room and the noise took Valentine from his trance; he closed his mouth and heard the noise of his teeth clicking then glanced at Colin. As the DI returned his gaze, the boy vanished.

'I'm sorry, Mr Stevenson. I find this very difficult, I know how much you have both been through.'

Marie leaned forward, a faint gleam entering her eyes. Colin patted her hand. 'Let the man speak, love.'

Valentine reached into his pocket and removed the small St Christopher pendant and instantly heard the ball bouncing in the hallway again. He kept his focus on Colin as he handed over the small pendant. 'Is this something you recognise?' he said.

Colin took the small piece of silver and passed it to his wife. The sound of the ball bouncing stopped once again and Rory appeared in the doorway. The boy looked at his mother holding the small pendant to her face and ran back to the hall. Marie Stevenson's cheekbones shone with tears as she buried her face in her husband's shoulder and cried for her lost son.

Colin spoke. 'This was Rory's.'

'Are you sure?' said Valentine.

'He got it from St John's. The initials are for the Cumnock Bible School. We've been looking for it for years. We thought we'd lost it too.'

The DI rose from his chair. He nodded briefly to DI McAlister and then turned back to face the Stevensons. 'We have quite a few more items down at the station. Do you think you'd be able to identify them?'

Colin dropped his head, once. 'Yes, we can come in tomorrow.'

'That would be very kind of you both.'

Colin stood up but kept his outstretched hand on his wife's shoulder. 'Will we get him back?'

For a moment Valentine didn't understand; his mind was a cleft of rock.

'We'd like to give him a Christian burial, Detective.'

'Yes, the remains will be released in due course.'

'Thank you.' A forced grin cut his face. He saw the officers out; his wife had returned into her silence once again.

In the street, Valentine removed his jacket and yanked off his tie, pulling the loop over his head. As he steadied himself on the garden wall he took deep gasps of the still air.

'Everything all right, boss?' said McAlister.

He felt energy seeping from the tensed stock of his body, like he had just sprinted farther and faster than he was capable of. His mind was constricting all thought again and confusion pervaded him. As he turned back to the Stevensons' home he caught sight of a small boy there. He was staring from an upstairs window. The DI felt a powerful connection to the boy, like he was communicating directly, and then his fingertips on the wall started to burn with a slow friction.

'Yes. I'm fine, Ally.' Valentine yanked away his hand and proceeded with quick footsteps back to the car.

'That was pretty intense in there,' said McAlister.

'You don't know the half of it!'

'Sir?'

'Nothing, Ally, I'm just rambling.'

'Looks like a positive ID.'

'That's a given. We won't get anyone to pick out Donal Welsh so confidently.'

'No, I shouldn't think so. He had no living relatives and

something tells me the remaining Columba staff will give it a wide berth.'

Valentine reached for his seat belt. 'Let's get back to the station. I want to see what's what with Garry Keirns.'

'He was released about an hour ago, sir. Phil phoned in. He says he can't find your other guy, the one from the original Columba House investigation.'

'Den Rennie? What's the problem there?'

'Apparently fishing on the Tweed, sir. He's somewhere in the Borders but nobody knows where. And no mobile either.'

'When's he due back?'

'I didn't get that far, boss.'

Valentine turned the key in the ignition. As he was pulling out a high-pitched cackle started to emanate from the radio.

'Bob, you hearing me?' It was Jim Prentice.

'Working late tonight again, Jimmy?'

'I put in more bloody hours than the rats down the docks.'

Valentine smirked into the mouthpiece. 'What can I do for you, mate?'

'I take it you're aware of the tailing operation on that wee scrote from Cumnock?'

The DI's attention lit up. 'Garry Keirns?'

'That's the one.'

'Yes, I gave the order. Is there some kind of problem?'

'Depends, where are you now?'

'I'm in Cumnock, Elizabeth Crescent.'

'OK, well I'll get DS Donnelly and DS McCormack to attend.'

Valentine glanced at McAlister – he shrugged and turned down the corners of his mouth. 'Jim, what's going on?'

'The two DCs on detail are saying things are kicking off – or to be more specific, your suspect is kicking off.'

Valentine put the car in gear and started to drive. 'Where?'

'A house on Racecourse Road.'

'I thought that was all hotels like the Savoy down there?'

'There's a few houses, for those that can afford them.'

'And whose house is this we're talking about?'

'This is the problem, Bob. It's a retired MP. We really need someone of your rank down there in case it gets out of hand. You know how these things have a nasty habit of finding their way into the papers.'

'A name please . . .' The DI was building up speed on the way back to Ayr.

'Fallon . . . Gerald Fallon.'

33

The street lamps painted a waxy orange glow on the road surface as Valentine pulled up in Racecourse Road. He spotted DS Donnelly's car in a side street adjacent to the large Victorian villa that detectives were surveying from beyond a high stone wall. He parked his car behind Donnelly's, and he and McAlister got out and jogged towards the others.

It was dark now, an amethyst haze covering the higher buildings of the town that made a dark and jagged horizon in the distance. The air was still and quiet; only whisperings could be heard beyond the wall, beneath the willow branches, where the detectives huddled.

'Phil, what's going on?' said Valentine.

The DS turned around. 'Oh, it's you. I thought it was Bill and Ben.'

'Who?'

'The woodentops the desk assigned to Keirns.' Donnelly pointed to a pale blue Mondeo that was parked over the road – two officers Valentine vaguely recognised sat inside.

'They're a bit wet behind the ears, that pair. Was there nobody else available?'

Donnelly shook his head. 'Apparently not.'

'I take it we've been brought out here on a wild goose chase?' said Valentine. McCormack and McAlister were exchanging frowns and head shakes.

'Well, that pair over there said it all kicked off, but when we got here all was quiet. I can see right into the front room and Keirns is there right enough, but he's calmed down.'

'What about the other one – Fallon?'

'He just brought Keirns a tumbler of something that looked like a wee goldie . . . it seems quite cosy.'

'Well, maybe it is now. Keep an eye on it.' Valentine turned from Donnelly and started for the Mondeo. He spotted the two detective constables inside looking away when they saw who was heading over.

Valentine tapped the driver's window. 'How's it going?'

'Hello, sir.' The constable appeared sheepish.

'Tell me what happened then.'

'Well, your big lad there arrived and ordered us to wait here.'

Valentine shook his head. 'I'm not on about that. Before DS Donnelly arrived, what was going on at the house?'

The man pulled himself up by the steering wheel and turned his face fully towards the detective. 'We were at Inkerman Court, the suspect's place . . .'

'Carry on.'

'And he came out, drove here. He was burning rubber, boss, and when he got out the face on him was not pretty.'

Valentine looked into the driveway. He spotted the Range Rover he'd seen at Sandy Thompson's funeral and recognised the number plate – GF 111. 'So where's Keirns's car?'

'Round at the old Pickwick. He strolled through, or should I say stomped. When he got to the front door there was a real flare-up, sir.'

A voice from the passenger's seat entered the conversation. 'It did, sir. We wouldn't have called it in otherwise – we're told to be very careful with the politicos.'

'You knew this was Fallon's place?'

'No. We asked the desk to check it – that's when we called it in.'

Valentine tapped the roof of the Mondeo. 'You did the right thing, lads. Better safe than sorry.'

'Thanks, boss.'

'Keep a close eye on him tonight. Oh and don't mind big Phil. His bark's worse than his bite.'

Valentine returned to the detectives in front of the wall that bordered Fallon's villa. McAlister was looking towards the large bay window that was well lit. Inside could clearly be seen the figures of Fallon and Keirns talking in front of a large open fireplace.

'False alarm,' said Valentine. 'Leave it to the young crew.'

'So that's it, sir?' said McAlister.

'Hardly. We go back to the station and leave the donkey work to the donkeys. We can be grateful for one thing though – this little incident has thrown up a very interesting set of possibilities. Not least being what in the name of Christ is Garry Keirns doing supping malt with Gerald Fallon?'

'I was wondering that myself, sir.'

'Well let's do some digging and find out because that's

two MPs that Keirns has managed to get very pally with. One I could almost believe was a strange act of chance, but two makes me think the absolute worst.'

Back at the station Valentine made straight for his office and checked his desk for memos. There was the usual smattering of junk, like CS Martin's call for overtime figures, and a missed call from Colleen in the press office just five minutes ago, but the one item of any interest was the memo from the lab.

'Shit,' said Valentine.

'Good news, sir?' said DS McCormack, entering the office and placing a folder on his desk.

'It's from the boffins. The bookie's pens are clean, not a single print.'

'Ouch. Guess we won't be hauling Keirns back in tonight then.'

'The night is young, Sylvia.' He pointed to the folder she'd just dropped. 'What's that?'

'The enlargement of the headless man's signet ring.'

Valentine opened the folder and peered inside. He closed it over just as quickly. 'When are we going to get a bloody break?'

'It's a stone, looks like garnet, might be a ruby,' said McCormack. 'It was probably too much to expect it to be initials, and even if it was it's unlikely they'd have been decipherable at this resolution.'

Valentine bit into the knuckles of his clenched fist. 'Let's try and be more optimistic. We have tonight's new lead to go on.'

DS Donnelly and DS McCormack walked into the room. McAlister informed them of the latest developments.

'So where do we go from here, sir?' said McAlister.

Valentine had swapped the knuckle of his right hand for a scalloped fingernail. He eased himself backwards to rest on the rim of his desk. 'Phil, keep chasing Den Rennie. What a bloody time to take a holiday.'

'Yes, sir.'

'And, Ally, I want you to run our esteemed friend Fallon through the mill. Any connection to Keirns or Columba in the members' interests, let me know. Trail all the usual sources too. If he cut a bloody ribbon for either of them I want to know. But most importantly I want to know where the late Andy Lucas fits in to all of this.'

'Lucas, sir?'

'Yes, by all accounts he just about walked away from his Cumnock seat at the height of his popularity. Why? And who, apart from Fallon, benefited from that? Means. Motive. Opportunity. Think about it. Rattle a few cages. With any luck the dirt on the bottom will land on someone we're after.'

'Yes, sir.'

The DI was pacing towards DS McCormack when he spotted the door of the incident room being pushed open.

'That's not a good sign.'

The detectives turned to face the oncoming figure of the station press officer.

'Colleen, isn't this a bit late for you?' said Valentine.

'Do you never check your messages?'

Valentine raised his hand in a gesture of surrender.

'If you did,' said Colleen, 'you'd know I've been trying to get you. My own phone has been ringing off the hook with

196

national reporters asking about the bodies of two young boys you uncovered in Cumnock.'

'I don't understand. We haven't released any information.'

Colleen dumped her bag on Valentine's desk and started to remove her jacket. 'I know that, because it would have come through me.'

'Then who?' said McCormack.

'Well fortunately I still have a few friends on the news desks, and I can confirm the source as a certain Freddie Gowan.'

'Gowan, the bastard!' said McAlister.

'A fair-enough assessment,' said Colleen. 'You could preface bastard with *disgruntled* going on the comments he's given reporters for tomorrow's papers.'

Valentine was breathing through widened nostrils. 'I should have known the minute he started complaining about losing money.'

Colleen folded her jacket over her arm and collected her bag from the desk. She was heading for the door when she spoke again. 'Right, hope none of you have any plans. This is going to be our war room for the next twenty-four hours . . . maybe longer.'

34

Wind chimes played in the breeze from one of the balconies of the luxury apartments. This part of the town, on the other side of the dock, had once been a wasteland. The only feature was a windswept and lonely fisherman's mission, but the building had been demolished long ago. It was debatable whether or not the gentrification process had improved the area or added anything to the coast other than the shelter of high-rise flats.

Valentine would occasionally stroll the streets around the station and down towards the shore front when the job conspired against him. It was easy to feel trapped inside the building after only a short time, and he'd just worked to the small hours and returned at first light. He needed to break away from the punishing constraints of the case and the now added pressure of unwanted media intrusion.

Sea birds circled overhead, squawking and sweeping down towards the low green to forage for abandoned chips, half-finished cones or whatever they could spy. The wind was low. A slight squall out at sea flushed the waves in steadily but slowly. The breezy sounds were soothing to the DI, who braced himself against a smirr of rain as he walked along the promenade.

He liked the elemental feel of the front, the touch of wind and rain on his face and the swirling, enveloping noise of the coast. He would often watch the sand moving on the dunes and feel his thoughts shifting with the seagrass. He had arrived here in a gloomy mood, the thought of how precious life was and how easily it was taken away uppermost. He thought of the two boys who had been murdered, and he weighed their loss against his own losses in life. There was no comparison.

Valentine had lived. He had had a life, and even if it had once come close to an abrupt ending with his near-fatal stabbing, he had held on to it. He wouldn't have missed anything if he had died, he thought. He'd lived his childhood, and almost all of his daughters' too. That would be his only regret if he was to shuffle off early: that his family would suffer.

But it gored Valentine to think of those two young lives, taken so early, before they had even had the chance to experience the world. Even if it was a dark place much of the time, it was still theirs too, and no one had the right to take that gift from them.

The DI sauntered back to the station, his hands stuffed in his pockets, his shoes pinching now with each heavy and tired step. When he opened the doors and walked in, his normal procedure was to address the desk, but on this occasion his attention was drawn in the opposite direction.

Sitting in a row of low-slung seats across from the counter were the Stevensons. Colin and Marie looked dressed for church, neat and prim. The DI knew it was just how they were – it was old school conditioning. In their eyes this was an occasion. It was a life event, even if it meant their only son would not be seen again.

'Hello there,' said Valentine.

Colin Stevenson rose from the seat and reached for the detective's hand. His wife remained silent and inscrutable.

The detective was about to lead them to the station's comfort room when DS McAlister appeared from the stairs with a blue folder under his arm. McAlister approached the group and addressed Valentine. 'This is the catalogue and the enlargements.'

'Thanks, Ally. I'll take it from here.'

The DI indicated the route through the swing doors to the right and proceeded to direct the Stevensons to a mid-sized room with cushioned chairs and a large coffee table; a small sink with cups in the drainer and a kettle sat nearby.

'Is there anything I can get you?' said Valentine.

'No, we're fine,' said Colin.

'Have you seen the newspapers today?'

'The papers? No. Why do you ask?'

Valentine pointed to the seating area. 'The case has attracted some attention. I dare say, in due course, they'll seek you out.'

'What would we have to say to the press?'

'You don't have to say anything if you don't want to.'

The couple crossed glances and Colin reached out to touch his wife on the elbow. 'Actually, can I nip to the loo, if you don't mind?'

She nodded and her husband left for the other end of the room where the toilets were signposted. The DI felt uncomfortable with the silent woman and realised he had yet to hear her say anything significant.

For a few moments, the room was completely still; it felt almost airless to Valentine, and then Marie Stevenson spoke.

'He's still with me,' she said.

Valentine was confused. Who was she talking about? 'I'm sorry?'

'Rory. He leaves me little signs.'

The DI smiled, as if that might be the end of the conversation.

'All the time,' said Marie. 'I didn't understand them at first, and then I saw a woman. She was sensitive, had a look in her eyes you might call knowing.'

'I see.' The DI walked over and sat down.

'I know I don't need to tell you, Mr Valentine.'

'You don't?'

Marie reached forward and gripped the detective's hand. 'I know,' she said. 'At first it was the pictures on the walls. They moved you know. Then the lights would flicker. But it was the dish rattling that made me understand.'

'The dish?'

'The little metal dish at the door, where we put the keys for the house. It rattled – still does – when I was close to it. She told me it was Rory, just letting me know he was there.'

Valentine nodded. He wasn't sure how to absorb the information.

Marie continued, 'It scared me a little, at first. But it's a comfort now. Do you understand?'

'Of course.'

'Yes. I know you do, Mr Valentine. I saw it in your eyes too.' She smiled, a thin, gentle smile. 'Thank you for finding my boy.'

201

Colin returned from the toilet and sat down beside the others. He was coughing into his fist as the DI drew the folder closer to them on the low table.

'I have some photographs I'd like to show you,' he said.

'Won't we see him?' said Colin.

'Not today. I'm afraid that won't be possible right away.'

The Stevensons started to grip each other like the night before. 'What do you have to show us, Detective?' said Colin.

Valentine opened the folder and placed some of the photographs on the table. They were the pictures taken by the SOCOs and the lab staff of the evidence retrieved from the murder scene.

The leather satchel. The rosary. A Sekonda watch. Black training shoes. A Spiderman comic. There were more items in the file, but the detective was aware of the Stevenson's change in demeanour.

Marie reached out for the picture of the satchel and withdrew her shaking hand. She touched her mouth and then buried her head in her husband's shoulder.

Colin nodded. 'These are our boy's.'

'Are you sure?' said Valentine.

'We picked out that watch for his birthday. I can still see his face when he put it on for the first time. It was just a silly little thing from Woolworth's . . . That's his rosary – his mother put it there, in the satchel every morning . . . Rory was Spiderman daft – there'd been a film on the television. You know how kids get. Another five minutes and he'd have been on to Batman or something else.'

Marie started to sob heavily now, her shoulders jerking

up and down with each cry. Colin put his arm around his wife. 'Will that be all, sir?'

'Yes. Thank you.' He picked up the pictures and shuffled them back into the folder.

Colin motioned Marie on to her feet.

The DI watched them struggle to the door, walking like a wounded beast, bound in misery. Valentine saw the couple back to the car park and offered to drive them to Cumnock but was rebuffed.

'Let us know when we can see Rory,' said Colin.

'I will.'

35

As he entered the incident room Valentine felt his shoulders tightening. The tension in the room was palpable, as if the temperature had been increased. As he looked around he caught sight of DS Donnelly at the photocopier and DS McAlister sitting at a desk, tapping the face of his watch. Everything appeared normal, and then his attention fell on the large windows of his corner office where the chief super was standing over a demure-looking DS McCormack.

As the DI entered his office McCormack turned away, crossing one leg over the other and beginning to delicately massage her knee. She looked awkward in the ensuing silence.

'Ah, Bob, were your ears burning you?' said CS Martin. 'We were just discussing you, but never mind, we can get back to that when you're out of the room.'

Valentine didn't move for the bait.

McCormack rose. 'I have some things to chase up.' She left the room, closing the door behind her.

'Take a seat, Bob,' said Martin.

'I'll stand, if you don't mind.'

'Oh, I don't mind at all what you do. Or perhaps what I

should say is I don't mind what you do so long as it's not splashed over the front pages of the newspapers.'

The DI eased himself on to the window ledge. 'I was waiting for this.'

'Waiting for what?'

'The ceremonial dressing down. Look, Freddie Gowan went to the papers because he's losing money on that bloody through road. I can't account for that kind of narrow-minded vindictiveness.'

Martin turned for the desk and snatched up a copy of the *Daily Record*. 'Yes, here we are . . . "The police are clueless, clutching at straws, pulling in myself and the former owner of the property, Mr Keirns, and making us spend a day waiting to be interviewed about nothing".'

Valentine squirmed. 'I recognise Freddie's quote.'

Martin threw down the paper. It slid off the desk with the force of the move. 'And unfortunately I recognise what he's bloody talking about, Bob.'

'Oh come on. That's unfair.'

'Is it? Well, how about this one then?' She picked up the Scottish edition of the *Express*. '"The police removed an old oil drum containing the bodies of two little boys they found on my land. It's a tragedy, but why aren't they doing anything about it? That's the real reason I've spoken out because people have the right to know."'

The DI started to gnaw on his lower lip.

'Nothing to say, Bob?' asked Martin. 'No explanation for that? Did you just disseminate the case details far and wide?'

Valentine stepped forward. 'Gowan's machinery found the oil drum, his workers had it open before we arrived. I can't gag everyone indefinitely. People talk, you know that.'

Martin returned to the desk, picking up papers and shouting out their titles at random before turning away and facing the DI. 'This is a train wreck, Bob. And it's only going to get worse. Colleen tells me there's been a TV helicopter out at the scene in Cumnock.'

'It might work to our advantage.'

'That's high optimism, Bob.' Martin laughed. 'It might work to your advantage given that you want out and the chief constable's been on to me already this morning.'

'Did he mention my transfer?'

'What do you think? Ask him your bloody self – I'm sure we'll be seeing him soon enough. So you might want to think about why you turned down his offer of help from the media unit. Because going by today's newspaper headlines I'd say that looks like a catastrophic lapse of judgement on your part.' Martin left, slamming the office door behind her.

Valentine returned to the window and watched as an oversized cloud crossed the sky, revealing a faint sun. The yellow rays the sun delivered settled on the surface of the River Ayr and left watery reflections dancing on the rippling surface. The scene did nothing to calm the detective's thoughts.

DS Donnelly was the first to emerge in the chief super's wake. 'Is it all clear, boss?'

'Yes, Phil, come in.'

DS McAlister and DS McCormack followed.

'Dino looks a bit agitated.'

'Don't worry about her – she likes to get worked up like that. It makes her feel important,' said Valentine.

'How did it go with the Stevensons?' said McAlister.

'It's a positive ID, as we predicted.'

'That's something. Phil has some more good news.'

'Phil?'

'Yes, the woodentops following Keirns have sent in their report from last night and there's some interesting stuff in there.'

'Go on . . .'

'Well, it seems after we left, another car turned up at Gerry Fallon's place, the occupant going in the house and making himself comfy with Keirns and Fallon for quite some time.'

'That's interesting,' said Valentine.

'It gets better,' said McCormack. 'I ran the number plate this morning and it belongs to a Glasgow man, Josh Simpson, who just so happens to be a freelance hack for hire with a nice sideline in political spin.'

'Really?'

'Yes, sir,' said McCormack. 'Now given that Garry Keirns has been quoted in three or four newspapers this morning, I think that's an interesting lead.'

'It's very interesting. Good work.' Valentine retrieved his car keys from the top drawer of his desk. 'Get your coat then, Sylvia.'

'Are we going to take Simpson in, sir?'

'You're kidding, aren't you? We're not interested in guns for hire. We're interested in Fallon.'

36

August 1984

My new friend is Rory Stevenson. He's ten and goes to St John's. I met him at the shop swapping football stickers. Rory has the most stickers – he has the Rangers badge, which nobody ever has. You never see the Rangers badge, or Kenny Dalglish, who plays for Liverpool. Rory supports Liverpool, and so do I now. I don't know why really. I don't know where it is even, but Kenny plays for them so they must be the best.

Rory says there's a football team for boys in the town. It's for under-twelves and he's going to play for them, and maybe I can too. There's trials soon and we're going together. The boys in the dorm don't like Rory. They don't like anyone that's not from the dorm because they call us tinkers and ask, 'Have you heard of soap?'

Rory doesn't say those things.

He's my best friend, and I don't know what I'd do without him.

Once we caught a frog. Just lying out on the grass, so it was. I picked it up and Rory put it in a brown-paper bag.

We walked with it down to the burn and let it go. We loved that frog.

On Sunday Rory has Bible class, but after we go roaming up the hills. We play *Star Wars* with sticks. I want to be Han Solo, but Rory says I can't be Solo because he doesn't have a lightsabre. Rory's good at finding sticks, though, so I go Vader and he goes Skywalker and we play lightsabres.

'It's getting late, we should go,' says Rory.

'No, stay out,' I say.

'I can't. My mam will be angry.'

We go back down the hill to the road and walk and walk forever, it seems.

'Who's that?' says Rory, pointing to a black car that's slowing down.

'Oh, Jesus.' I know straight away who it is.

'What is it?'

'Run. Run for your life, Rory.' We take off running along the road, just hoping for a gap to appear that we can jump through into a field and away from the black car, but there's no gaps.

The man in the black car opens the door and sends out the dorm boys, who come running and pin us down. They smell of chocolate and crisps and are mad wild with the excitement of it all.

'Get off, y'bastards!' I shout. I can hear Rory shouting too, but I can't make out the words.

They put us in the car and drive away. It's dark now, properly dark. I get a dead arm every time I move and every time I try to talk to Rory. The boys are yelling and jumping about, and it's burning hot inside the car, so much that a window has to be opened.

'Shut it,' says the driver man. I know him from before – I recognise the pig eyes. After a while, once the messing stops, the man says, 'Have some pop with your pals.' I say no but Rory takes one and I tell him, 'No, it's poison.' I remember the last time I had the pop, the woozy feeling and the sickness. I want to let Rory home to his mam, because I know where the man with the pig eyes will take us.

'Donal, where are we?' says Rory in a whisper.

'Shhhh . . . we'll get leathered.'

'I have to go. My mam will be mad.'

'Rory, keep quiet. We'll find a chance and run away. I promise, I promise you that.'

The car goes up hill again, then down and turns and turns again, and I think this must be the twistiest, windiest road in the world ever. There's a light up ahead now; when we get nearer I see it's on a house, like a farm. The car stops with a jerk.

'Here we are, kiddies!' says the man with pig eyes. 'In you go now, to the party.'

I see Rory looking at me when the man says party, and I want to tell him 'no, no, it's not that sort of party' but he walks in with the others and doesn't say a word.

Inside the lights are low and there's all kinds of cakes about the place. It's hot with the great, big roaring fire, and there's lots of men with ties and suits and shiny buckles on their belts. I get caught up in the rush through the door, and then there's a sound of boys shouting and more music, and I wonder where Rory is so I call out to him, but he's nowhere to be seen.

'Rory . . . Rory . . .' I say.

'Calm your ardour!' says a man with yellow teeth and a cigarette between his fingers. He's old and has white hair flattened to the top of his head, but his shirt is open to the waist, and I can see his braces over his belly.

'Rory . . . where are you?' I yell out.

He doesn't reply, and I start to run about the house looking for him. I open the closed doors, and a man says something in a posh voice, and then I try another door, but there's only a boy lying on the floor crying. I say 'Rory' again and again, but I get no reply – and then I hear a scream, and I know at once the sound of that voice.

He's behind a patchy blue door, upstairs at the end of the landing where the carpet has started to wear away. I rush to the door but it's stuck, and I have to heave and push and throw myself about to get it open, but when I get inside I see Rory in the corner with his satchel up over his face.

He's crying and roaring out for his mam, but the man is only shouting back and slapping him on the side of the head when he can reach him. The man is tall, bigger than Rory by a mile, and he's swaying about with the drink in him.

'Get away! Leave him,' I say.

'Who the hell . . .'

I run at him with my fists flying, and I hit him in the stomach, but the man pushes me out of the way. I run again and he kicks out, but his trousers fall and his leg catches in the roll of the fabric. He sways for a moment, and then he knocks Rory to the floor. Rory stays down, he doesn't move and I wonder is he even breathing. I run over and his eyes are closed, but he coughs and splutters a little and I know he's fine.

'Come on, Rory, we have to go!' I try to pick him up, so we can run away, but he's too heavy, and then I feel someone lifting me and I'm pushed again, and I'm flying to the bed.

I see the man coming for me. His eyes are wide and his nose is bloody. He throws himself on top of me and puts his hands on my neck. I try to kick him, but my legs are pinned.

I try to hit out, but my arms are stuck fast.

I look to the floor and see Rory and I try to say, 'Run, Rory,' but I can't even move my lips now.

I see him, my best friend, just lying there. And I start to cry. The tears are cold on my warm cheeks but they don't last for long.

37

At Alloway Place the traffic lights changed, allowing the cars backed up Miller Road to cross the detectives' path. Valentine checked the clock on the dashboard and began to feel the familiar tightness of tension in his shoulders. There was anger in there too, the kind that was hard to suppress, but he knew he would have to batten it down if he was to get anywhere with Fallon.

The trail of cars halted in the middle of the road as the lights changed again – it looked like they were going nowhere fast.

'Bloody hell,' said Valentine.

'It's always the same at this end of the town,' said DS McCormack.

'You realise you're beginning to sound like a local. You'll be singing the virtues of the Electric Bakery next.'

'Eh, no, I don't think so. I'd like to still be able to sprint after the odd scrote when required.'

Valentine smiled. He felt his temper cooling. The car in front moved forward a couple of lengths, just in time for the detectives to be caught as the lights changed again.

'How have you been, boss?' said McCormack. 'Our paths haven't crossed a lot these last few days.'

'Have you been talking to Ally?'

'No. Why?'

'No reason.' Valentine put the driver's window down a few inches. 'Just me being paranoid.'

'I take it something happened at the Stevensons' place?'

Valentine stared out the window at a man with a dog.

McCormack spoke again. 'I'll take that as a yes then. It wasn't like our visit to Janie Cooper's parents, was it?'

The lights changed. The DI was grateful for the opportunity to avoid the conversation.

As he put the car in gear and pulled out McCormack pressed him. 'Well, boss?'

'No, Sylvia. There was no threat from Ally to call an ambulance if that's what you're getting at.'

'I sense a but . . . there's a *but* coming, isn't there?'

'But it was a similar scenario.'

'You saw him? Rory.'

They'd crossed the junction and were heading down Racecourse Road in a slow procession. The man walking the dog had made further progress than the officers in the car.

'It wasn't the same. The Cooper girl was like a shock, a jolt. I didn't feel that way this time.'

'Well, how did you feel?'

'Perfectly calm. That was until . . .'

'Yes?'

The car started to move again. They pulled up outside the address Valentine had attended previously. 'This is it, isn't it?'

'You know it is, Bob. Tell me what happened.'

He cut the engine but continued to hold tightly to the

steering wheel and the gearstick. 'The next day, Marie, the boy's mother, she said she knew.'

'Holy . . . you mean she saw?'

Valentine shrugged. 'I don't know, sensed maybe. She told me so.'

'She just came out with it?'

'More or less. I think it was a comfort to her, like she felt something. I don't know, Sylvia, I'm still trying to get my head around the fact that this is happening to me. It's too much to process without trying to think of the fact that I'm not alone – that there's others who can tune in to this stuff.'

'Crosbie said it was very common, that to a greater or lesser degree we could all do it.'

'Did he?'

'Yes.' McCormack followed Valentine out of the car. On the pavement they continued to talk. 'I see a big change in you, sir. You're getting to grips with this now.'

'How do you know I'm not just getting good at hiding it?'

'I'm trained to catch liars, that's why.'

'Maybe I'm better than you think.'

'Maybe you're better than you think.'

The detectives stalled outside the large Victorian sandstone, staring up at the bay window where they had watched Keirns the first night they'd attended. It seemed some distance from the gated driveway and lawns attached to the property. As they drew nearer to the house, Valentine saw the front door was open, and he could hear voices inside.

'At least someone's home,' he said.

As he passed the Range Rover, he noticed the rear door

215

of the vehicle had been pulled wide. A small weekend bag sat in the hollow interior, with what looked like a gun carrier down the side.

'Hang on,' said Valentine.

'What is it?'

He reached into the vehicle and removed the gun case. As he unzipped the front end, a rifle point protruded.

'Careful now,' shouted a voice from the steps. It was Fallon. He was dressed for the outdoors in green wellingtons and dark corduroys; a wax jacket sat over a red V-neck and driving gloves covered his hands.

'It's not loaded,' said Valentine.

'Of course not.' Fallon descended the steps and threw his jacket in the back of the vehicle. 'I wasn't expecting a visit from the police.'

'How do you know we're police?' said Valentine.

Fallon grinned. 'Who else would stand and look at a brand-new Browning as if it was guilty of a heinous crime. I have a licence, you know, just getting ready for the Glorious Twelfth!'

'I'm not here to inspect your licence.' The detectives introduced themselves and were directed inside by the owner of the property. In the hallway, by a winding baluster rail, Fallon shouted to some boisterous dogs beyond a door, 'Let them run out the back, we have some visitors.'

'We won't take up much of your time, Mr Fallon.'

'It's perfectly all right – my wife will calm the dogs down. They get excited at the sight of the boots – think we're going out.'

Fallon led the officers into a long lounge room. At one end, full-length chintz curtains hung either side of a large bay window that took in the view of the garden and gates. In the middle, a white mantle supported an ornamental clock that was flanked by silver candlesticks. There was a broad picture opposite in a gilt frame, portraying a scene of men in red hunting jackets riding horseback over a green countryside. A long table at the other end of the room was covered with a messy pile of newspapers that looked out of place in the pristine home.

'Can I offer you a drink, officers?' said Fallon.

'That won't be necessary.'

'Please, take a seat.'

Valentine remained standing, where he could view the stock of newspapers in the reflection of a mirror hanging above the fireplace. He let his gaze linger long enough for Fallon to register his interest.

'How can I help you?' said Fallon. He unbuttoned the supporting strap on his gloves but didn't remove them.

'Do you always buy every newspaper on the stand, Mr Fallon?' Valentine turned away and walked towards the table. When he reached the pile of papers, he saw they all seemed to be open at the same story.

'No, I was alerted to this particular point of interest by a former constituent of mine.'

Valentine picked up the first paper he saw and handed it to DS McCormack. 'Exactly what interest do you have in my current murder investigation?'

Fallon placed his hands behind his back. 'I was the MP for the area for many years, Detective.'

'Is that your answer?'

'Isn't it good enough for you?'

Valentine watched McCormack fling the paper back

217

on the table. The noise distracted the retired MP.

'Why are you here, Mr Valentine?' said Fallon.

Valentine ignored the question and started to wander around the table, looking at the various newspaper spreads. 'Not exactly a story you'd want to be reminded of for the purposes of nostalgia, is it?'

'Nostalgia's not what it used to be,' Fallon joked.

'The death of two young boys isn't a laughing matter, Mr Fallon.'

'Surely you don't think I have anything to do with that?'

Valentine left his question hanging, once again.

'How do you know Garry Keirns?' he said.

'Mr Keirns was a constituent of mine.'

'Play host to a lot of your former constituents regularly, do you?'

Fallon took a step closer to the detectives. 'Look, what is this all about?'

'I'll ask the questions, Mr Fallon – that's generally the way it goes in murder investigations. Now, Garry Keirns – why was he here?'

Fallon turned towards the mantle and made a show of removing his gloves. He placed them beside the clock. 'He asked me for some advice on a private matter.'

'And just how can *public* relations be a private matter, Mr Fallon?'

'What?'

'I'm referring to Josh Simpson, the hack and political press man who was running your little media hub from here.' Valentine waved a hand towards the table piled with newspapers.

Fallon put his hands in his pockets and shrugged, forcing

his shoulders to square broadly. His gaze roved over the two officers standing in his home. 'On whose authority are you here, Mr Valentine?'

'I'm sorry, I don't understand the question.'

'Well maybe I can spell it out in simpler terms for you. Does your chief constable know you are here?'

'Why would he?'

'Exactly what I thought. William Greaves would be far too circumspect to vouch for this kind of fishing expedition. Perhaps I should give him a call now.'

Valentine turned to face DS McCormack, whose expression was dominated by the small hollow of the pointed mouth in the centre of her face.

'Detective Inspector Valentine is in charge of this investigation,' said McCormack.

'Oh, she speaks,' mocked Fallon. 'I suppose that's two names I'll have to raise with Mr Greaves now. He's going to be busy with the carpetings.'

'If that's supposed to be some kind of threat . . .' McCormack paused to gather steam, but Valentine raised a hand to calm the DS and returned to the former MP.

'Threatening a police officer – comical though it is to be threatened with an old school tie – is a serious offence, Mr Fallon,' said the DI.

Fallon's face ruptured into laughter. 'I'm sorry if I gave you that impression, Detective Inspector Valentine. It's just that I am far more used to speaking to the organ grinder than his little monkey.'

Fallon placed a hand on Valentine's shoulder and proceeded to tap gently. He was halfway towards the third tap in succession, guffawing noisily in the DI's face, when

Valentine grabbed his hand and turned it behind his back, meeting the wrist with a set of handcuffs.

'I'm arresting you, Mr Fallon. You don't have to say anything . . .'

The laughter halted. 'Arresting me! On what charge?'

'But anything you do say may be written down and used in evidence . . .'

'Now hang on.' He struggled with the restraints as his face darkened and thick veins grew in his neck. 'Just where do you find the gall to march into my home making all kinds of ludicrous assumptions?'

'Have you even the slightest idea how serious disrupting a murder investigation is? I came here to give you the chance to explain yourself, but you seem determined only to undermine my authority. We could have done this quietly, on your own terms, but you are eager to make a trip to the station.'

'OK, proceed, Detective.' Fallon straightened himself. 'I've a feeling *serious* and *disruption* are two words you're going to become very familiar with quite soon.'

38

As DI Valentine closed the back door of the car on Gerald Fallon he made his way around the vehicle, where he was met by DS McCormack. The former MP's large home sat defiantly behind them, a looming presence that seemed to disapprove of their actions. As Valentine tried to step around the DS, she stopped him with the flat of her hand and drew out a sour look that made the detective retreat a few steps.

'What's all this?' said Valentine.

'I could ask you the same thing,' said McCormack. 'Are you actually on the lookout for trouble now?'

'Oh come on, Sylvia. Fallon's dicking us around and you know it as well as I do.'

She gripped the leather strap of her bag. 'I'm thinking about the outcome, boss.'

'So am I. We could spend all day playing footsie under the table with him in the hope that he deigns to give us something.'

'And this is going to get us a result faster, is it?'

'Yes. Because I intend to rip it out of him.' Valentine walked around the DS, lunging for the door handle on the car.

They didn't speak again until they reached the station. As the car passed the front door, Valentine spotted a group of press photographers sitting on the steps. He checked in the rear-view mirror to see that Fallon had seen them too. He had, his face hardening as he glanced over the high bridge of his nose. He sat in silence until the car was parked at the back entrance.

Valentine opened the car door for Fallon, but the retired MP waited, straightening his cuff and fanning a lapel before he emerged. As he readied himself for what was to come, a truculent gleam entered his eye. 'You're opening a can of worms, Detective.'

The DI declined to respond. 'Get Mr Fallon booked into an interview room, DS McCormack.'

'Yes, sir.'

'I'll be with you shortly.'

Valentine didn't look back as he headed through the entrance and up the stairs to the incident room. He had a niggling feeling that the chief super might be nosing about and that she would scupper his plans to grill Fallon.

Upstairs, his mind ran a program of responses he might give to Martin, but she wasn't there. The DI approached Donnelly. 'No sign of Dino?'

'She was in earlier, throwing the newspapers about and grumbling. How did the Fallon visit go?'

'About as well as expected.' He picked up an empty file and started to fill it with papers and photographs. 'I see we have a three-ring media circus camped out on the front steps.'

'Colleen's doing her nut in the press office, says the phone hasn't stopped.'

Valentine groaned audibly. 'And it's only going to get worse.'

'How come?'

'Just trust me on that.' He tucked the folder under his arm and tapped down the stray contents. 'No sign of Den Rennie yet?'

'I'm afraid not, boss.'

'Well, keep at it. As soon as you get hold of him, call him in. I don't care if we have to pick up taxi fare from bloody Kelso.'

The DI made his way back downstairs. At the custody counter the desk sergeant's eyes twitched over the pages of the *Daily Record* newspaper. He seemed engrossed in the report, his head clamped at a tight angle to the two-page spread. He didn't look up as Valentine appeared.

'What room's DS McCormack in?'

'Oh, sorry, sir . . . number three.'

'Thanks.'

The officer indicated the newspaper. 'Those two wee boys, just shocking.'

Valentine nodded – avoiding comment – and made for the interview room. DS McCormack was seated inside facing Fallon. He was straight-backed but seemed impatient, his fingernails chamfering at the edge of the table.

The DI put down the folder and removed his chair. When he sat he let his fingers rest on the papers. 'Tell me again about your association with Garry Keirns please.'

'I told you already, he was a constituent of mine.' Fallon's voice was edged with condescension.

'Indulge me with the details.'

Fallon sighed. 'He was very active in the community,

223

lots of groups and so on. I believe that's how he first came to my attention.'

'How close did you become?'

'*What?* We didn't become close at all.'

Valentine reached into the blue folder and placed a piece of paper in front of Fallon. 'Do you recognise this?'

'It looks like a reference. It's not from my office.'

'Your predecessor, Andrew Lucas.'

Fallon pushed away the paper. 'I'm not accountable for Andy Lucas.'

'I'm not suggesting you are. Can you read the reference and let me know if it corresponds to your opinion of Garry Keirns?'

Fallon removed a thin case from his pocket containing reading glasses and picked up the paper once more. 'It looks a little over the top, a little la-di-da . . . Andy was like that.'

'So you don't agree with Mr Lucas's impression of Keirns?'

'What does my opinion matter? I'm not either man's keeper.'

'I'm trying to establish what kind of a relationship you had with Mr Keirns, who happens to be a person of interest in our murder investigation, and with whom you appear sufficiently acquainted to invite into your home late at night to avail himself of your media contacts.'

'Now hang on a minute.'

'No, you hang on, Mr Fallon. Now the question is, do you recognise the Garry Keirns that your predecessor Andy Lucas seemed so very fond of?'

'No.' He dipped his chin. 'I don't recognise him. It looks

like the kind of reference that would be written with a distinct purpose in mind.'

'Such as?'

'I don't know, to help a planning application or something. It's glowing so much it's incandescent. How could it represent anyone accurately?'

Valentine picked up the reference and returned it to the folder. 'Thank you, Mr Fallon.' The two men appraised each other over the table for a moment. 'Why do you think Andy Lucas would put his name to lies about Garry Keirns?'

'Oh come on.'

'You've said yourself the reference is inaccurate.'

'Yes but lies? He's dead now, you know.'

'Suicide, wasn't it?'

'I believe so.'

'You don't sound so sure. Created quite a job opportunity for you, Mr Lucas's death, didn't it?'

Fallon shook his head and let his gaze rest on the floor. 'This really is the most ridiculous . . .'

'You must have been very grateful to Andrew Lucas. He handed you the largest majority in the country when he died.'

'You'll be saying he was responsible for my holding the seat for all those years next.'

Valentine leaned forward. 'Not at all, Mr Fallon. I'm quite sure it takes a particularly skilled kind of individual to hold political office for that length of time.'

Fallon stood up. 'I'm not staying here to be insulted, even by insinuation. Either charge me with whatever trumped-up piece of jaywalking legislation you have on me, or release me now.'

DS McCormack rose. 'Please sit down, Mr Fallon.'

'No. This is ludicrous. I've had enough. What the hell does any of this have to do with the death of two boys thirty-odd years ago?'

Valentine raised his voice. 'I was just coming to that. Now sit down please.'

Fallon drew back his seat again. 'This better be good.'

'You were a patron of Columba House for Boys in Cumnock I believe?'

'Yes. But I wasn't alone.'

'No, that's true. Two of the people we've been discussing already – Garry Keirns and Andrew Lucas – were also patrons.'

'What of it?'

'You'll be aware of the tawdry demise that met Columba House.'

'I could hardly ignore it, being as it was in my constituency.'

'True. And given that you have already demonstrated your willingness to extend services above and beyond the call of duty to your constituents, perhaps you'd like to tell me what favours were asked of you at the time of the abuse scandal?'

'Absolutely none.' He tapped his index finger on the tabletop. 'And I say that categorically.'

'And what about Andy Lucas?'

'What about him?'

'He committed suicide soon after the investigation that closed Columba House.'

'I don't follow your tangent, Detective.'

'No. Well, let me explain it for you. There were

twenty-nine Columba boys abused by – we're led to
believe – four men. I think that's an imbalance. Maybe
some got away.'

Fallon cleared all expression from his face. His cheekbones sat firm and prominent above an unmoving mouth.

'I suppose what I'd like to ask you now, Mr Fallon, is
about Garry Keirns. Does he always come to you with his
problems?'

Fallon shook his head.

Valentine opened the file again and removed the photograph of the boy and his abuser taken from beneath the
floorboards in Keirns's former home. The DI stared at the
picture for a few seconds before handing it over to Fallon.

'Do you recognise the man in this photograph, Mr Fallon?'

39

Fallon bent over the picture, bunching his brows. He stared solidly and dispassionately before picking up his glasses once more and drawing the picture towards him. He reviewed the scene closely, his broad forehead creasing as his gaze roved.

Valentine recorded his reaction, waiting for any telling signs that might betray Fallon. His breathing was steady, his pallor unchanged, but as he removed his glasses and pushed away the picture his voice trailed into a dull monotone.

'I'd like to – I mean, can we have an interval?' said Fallon.

'Why?'

'I need time to . . .' He smoothed the edges of his lips with his finger and thumb.

Valentine reached for the photograph. He held it up. 'Has something here jogged your memory, Mr Fallon?'

'No, that's not it.'

'Don't tell me it's your conscience?'

Fallon looked away, sinking into his chair. He appeared shrunken before the officers; his ferocity diminished.

Valentine slapped down the picture. 'You know who this is – don't you?'

The DI rose from his chair and went to stand next to Fallon. The former MP raised a dismissive hand, but the gesture said more about how his energy had been sapped. He became twitchy, scratching the corner of his nose then touching the seam of his jumper before staring at his hands like he didn't know what to do next with them.

The door to the interview room opened and DS Donnelley lunged towards the officers. 'Boss, we need you right away.'

'Not now, Phil.'

'Sir, we've found him.'

'Den Rennie?' The name sent a jolt through Fallon.

'Yes.'

'I'm coming.'

In the corridor Valentine turned to face DS McCormack. 'Fallon's on the ropes.'

'It's the photo – he knows something.'

'Getting it out of him will be the hard bit. But that's not all he knows.'

'You mean Rennie?'

Valentine's gaze flitted. 'You saw it too?'

'It definitely registered, sir.'

The officers ascended the stairs with something like optimism raising them up. In the incident room DS McAlister beckoned to Valentine with a raised hand; in his other hand he indicated a telephone receiver.

'That him?' said the DS.

Valentine took the phone and gave his name and rank. The exchange was brief, but the detective was absorbed in the words. The team around him was soaking up the information.

He put the receiver back in the cradle.

'He's here.'

'In Ayr?' said McAlister.

'Not quite. Fenwick. I told him to stay there. I'm going out now.'

The officers started to reach for coats and keys. 'No, it's not a field trip. I'm going alone.'

'Are you sure, sir?' said DS McCormack.

'He wants our chat to be off the record, so I'm going alone.'

'OK,' said McCormack. 'We're here if you need us.'

'I'm sure I won't. But keep an eye on Fallon. I don't think he's in a good place right now.'

'Best place for him.'

Valentine grinned.

In the car the DI went over his thoughts, which seemed to sit somewhere between the blackening clouds that hung overhead and whatever lay beyond. When the rain broke it was little surprise that it shot at the windscreen like javelins, bouncing off the bonnet and the road incessantly.

By Fenwick the downpour had settled into a persistent drizzle and the potholes of the road spilled over with oily waters. At the pub car park a downpipe overflowed the drain, causing a wet apron to cover the pavement. The DI had to dance around the splashes as he entered the building.

A stooped man in a navy-blue Berghaus jacket was waiting by the doorway. He seemed agitated, playing with the change in his pockets as he waited with cheeks so pinched he looked like he might spit.

'Valentine?' he said.

'Hello, Den.' The men shook hands and made their way through to a quiet area of the bar. They exchanged pleasantries about the poor weather and Rennie's recent fishing trip, which he had interrupted before taking anything that might qualify as a trophy catch.

'I'm very grateful for this, Den,' said Valentine.

'I hear it was on the news, the old case.'

'I rarely catch the news in this job.'

'You're not missing much. It was the paper I saw.'

The waitress brought over their drinks on a tartan tray and set them down on the tabletop.

'I wasn't going to come,' said Rennie.

'Why not?'

He picked up his drink. 'Before we speak, I need to know where you're coming from.'

'I don't understand.'

'I mean, are you going to get to the bottom of this?'

Valentine watched Rennie sip his drink. The gaze was returned in full.

'I know about Pollock, if that's what you're hinting at. I know he was a blow-in who suddenly appeared and stuck a nice, neat bow on everything.'

Rennie nodded. 'Then buggered off to Spain, never to be seen or, more importantly, heard from again.'

The DI sensed a note of bitterness, of unfinished business. For the next few moments he assured Rennie of his desire to get to the truth about the two murdered boys he had unearthed in a barrel, of how he had met the Stevensons, Keirns, Fallon and of his suspicions about Lucas and what went on at Columba House. The mention of the retired detective's former case seemed to sour him further.

'And you think they're going to let you solve this, do you?' said Rennie.

'How can anybody stop me?'

He started to laugh. 'You've really no idea, have you?'

'Perhaps you should fill me in.'

He returned to the spluttering laugh. 'You mean before they do?'

'Who's *they*?'

The laughter subsided. Rennie straightened himself in his chair and spoke slowly. 'Let me tell you a little story about the days when I sat where you are sitting now.'

'Go on.'

'The week before Pollock was brought in I had a very interesting chat with my chief constable, and do you know what he said? He told me that, sometimes, investigations like this one do not end. I was flabbergasted, I didn't know what he was on about, and then he explained himself. He said sometimes investigations do not reach a logical conclusion, ever, and if this case falls into that category no one will question it again.'

Rennie let the remark sit between them for a moment and then returned to his subject. 'Bob, when I heard that, it didn't have the intended impact on me.'

'You were supposed to shut up.'

'I know that, and you know that. But for some reason I ignored the warning, I just carried on as if nothing had happened. In fact, I might even have upped my game a little, started to talk a little too loudly.'

'How did that play out?' said Valentine.

'Pretty much how you'd expect. I saw press stories refuting forensic tests before the lab had even done them. I had witness statements retracted. The machinery was put to work against me.'

'What were they refuting? What was being hidden?'

'Everything. You know about Andy Lucas?'

'You spoke out about his suicide in the papers.'

'Suicide?' Rennie spat the word. 'His neck was broken long before someone arranged for it to go in that noose.'

'You had evidence?'

'Of course we did. The skin folds were inconsistent with the angle of the break. The noose only rolled the dead skin on the bone. But none of this was ever reported.'

'Certainly not after Pollock took over the case.'

'Started his bloody whitewash you mean.' Rennie shook his head. 'What did they get? Four including the master, Healey? There were gangs of them raping boys and we had nigh on sixty boys telling us that.'

'Only four convictions.'

'Like I said, a farce. Columba House was a bloody factory supplying those boys on a conveyor belt. They were picked up and passed around like toys, ferried about from hotel to country house . . . It disgusted me. I've seen some stuff in this racket, but that really sickened me for life.'

'Why didn't you speak out at the time?' Valentine's remark sounded like an accusation.

'How could I by then? Everything they printed in the papers was controlled – it was all run like clockwork. Who'd believe me? Me against the chief constable, against the magistrate and the MPs? It went all the way to the top. They told me that, Bob – the top.'

'You can talk now.'

'Do you think the case files even exist now?'

'You can make a statement, on the record.'

Rennie clamped his teeth shut and exhaled slowly through thinned lips. 'I did all I could to get those bastards when I was in a position to try. What makes you think anything's changed?'

'Times have changed, Den.'

'No they haven't. You might think they have because a few big shots have been found out, but that's all part of the plan, like Healey. Someone has to suffer for the rest to survive. This is going nowhere. Your investigation's going nowhere, because if it did, we'd have to tear up the world and start again from scratch.'

40

Valentine awoke from disturbing dreams to a reality that seemed every bit as horrific. Clare was gone from his side. She was always an early riser, but he had heard her waken in the small hours and retreat downstairs. At the time, he had thought to follow her, but weary limbs and a heavy head kept him slumped in the bed. He thought again about that now and wondered if he had done the right thing. Like so much else involving his wife, he decided only time would tell.

He rose and showered, got dressed and struggled with the knot of his tie for several minutes. It seemed either too big or too small and never quite attained the optimum balance between opposing ends. For a moment he trialled the idea of giving up, perhaps wearing an open collar, but it didn't feel right.

In the kitchen, Clare sat at the breakfast bar staring on to the lawn. When he looked out the window her gaze was falling on nothing more than the bird table and the shamefully ignored decking with its dulled varnish. She seemed distant, and he knew why.

'Morning, love,' he said.

'Oh, you're up. I didn't see you there.' Some husbands

would have asked what was wrong, prodded her for answers, but that wasn't Valentine's way. He knew any answer he received would be forced and far away from the truth. There'd been enough conflict at home recently, and all he wanted was a ceasefire.

'Coffee?' said Valentine.

Clare shook her head and put down her cup. 'This transfer, Bob . . .'

'Not now, love.'

'Well when?'

He filled the kettle from the tap. Too much pressure sprayed water on the wall tiles. 'Soon. I've made the request – it's out of my hands now.' Valentine tried to make light of the matter, stepping away from the kettle and collecting his mobile phone from the shelf next to the fridge where he always kept it.

He was scrolling through a list of new messages when he felt Clare squeeze past him on her way to the stairs.

'Clare . . .'

'I'm going for a shower.' The words sounded matter of fact, innocent even, but backed with her actions they told Valentine his wife was running out of patience.

The latest message on his phone was from DS McAlister, delivered at close to midnight. Three previous messages were sitting there from McAlister too. The detective was opening the first message when the phone started to ring.

'Hello, Ally,' said Valentine.

'Finally. You've been incommunicado.'

'Hardly. I checked in with the office before I went to bed last night and all was quiet on the western front.'

'Didn't your wife pass on my message?' McAlister sounded flustered and Valentine parried the question.

'I had a hell of a lot to think about last night – I crashed out. Look, what's up, Ally?'

'Eh, I don't quite know where to start.'

'How about the beginning?'

'Well, that would be when the chief constable showed, I suppose.'

'Bill Greaves came to the station?'

'It gets better – or should that be worse?'

'I can't think how but go on.'

McAlister's voice came low and rasping over the phone. 'Well, Greavsie did his nut about Fallon being in custody and demanded we release him.'

'Oh shit.'

'That's not the worst bit, boss. I signed Fallon out and handed him over to uniform because there was only me left on – and the DCs tailing Garry Keirns.'

Valentine sensed a placatory excuse unfurling. 'Go on, Ally.'

'Well, uniform were taking Fallon home, but they took him out the front door . . .'

'Tell me there wasn't still press there.'

McAlister paused. 'I assume you haven't seen the papers.'

Valentine felt the phone weighing heavy in his hand. 'They got him, I take it?'

'There could only have been one snapper hanging on. He must have wired it to the news desks, boss.'

'You're right, that's worse, Ally.'

'Sorry, sir, but that's not all.'

'Spit it out then.'

'Garry Keirns is dead.'

Inkerman Court's one entrance road was sealed with blue and white tape when Valentine arrived. He motioned to a uniform in a high-vis vest and asked him to lower the tape. As the DI drove to the parking area – a small strip of road squeezed between a sparse patch of green belt and the municipal swimming baths – he spotted DS Donnelly directing the operation.

'Phil, over here,' yelled Valentine.

'Boss . . .'

'What's the SP?'

'There was no movement after lights out so the DC on the handover took a closer look. And saw Keirns's Hush Puppies swinging in the hallway when he looked through the letterbox.'

'Do we have the time of death?'

'He's been cold for nine or ten hours, they say.'

'And Bill and Ben saw nothing?'

'They were watching his car and the front door.'

'What about the back door?'

'It's a bloody rabbit warren around here. You'd have to go through the close and sit in the courtyard to even see the back door. You couldn't get a car round there.'

'And of course nobody thought to do that?'

Donnelly shrugged and Valentine headed for the property.

The hallway was small. A cramped staircase led on to further floors. On the ground level was a little laundry room, a bedroom with patio doors and a further corridor leading to the back door. In the garden, DS McAlister and DS McCormack were standing with the SOCOs. Everything was viewable from one point in the vestibule, where Valentine was forced to ease himself into the hallway and around the dangling corpse of Garry Keirns as he headed for the other officers.

'Cometh the hour . . .' said McAlister.

'Pack it in,' said Valentine. 'Any marks on those doors?'

'Multiple scratches on the patio-door frames,' said McCormack. 'The door at the back has had the lock jemmied at some point, but it's a new lock. The neighbours say it was a rental property for a number of years, and there were a few tenants that didn't look after it.'

'So we've two potential entrance points.'

McCormack nodded. 'Looks that way.'

Valentine walked to the end of the path, keeping his voice low. 'Any footprinting?'

'There's been heavy rain, sir. Most of it'll be washed away.'

The DI stood on the balls of his feet and stared into the open door at the rear of the property. He could still see the swaying corpse of Garry Keirns hanging from the banister at the end of the hallway.

'A nice clean job, eh?' said Valentine.

'You're not entertaining suicide, sir?' said McAlister.

'Oh do me a favour. Keirns had been potless his whole life. He just gets his hands on some money and he does himself in?'

'Maybe he felt pressured?' said McCormack.

'Do you know what I think? I think somebody else felt pressured.' Valentine pushed away from the officers and

239

marched back up the path towards the house. At the back door he turned. 'Get him down now and get the remains to Wrighty. And tell him to have a bloody close look, because if there's any doubt, we call this murder.'

Valentine drove through the blue and white tape on his way from the crime scene. At the station there seemed to be more press than ever on the front steps, and their number had been added to by a flash protest mob waving placards and shouting.

'What the hell is that?' said the DI. He had never known King Street station to be picketed, and he knew the top brass wouldn't be pleased.

In the car park the detective spotted the chief constable's Lexus parked outside the rear entrance to the building. He tried not to imagine what kind of conversation Bill Greaves might be engaged in with the chief super, but he couldn't shake the image of a red-faced Greaves spewing fire.

Valentine avoided the usual pleasantries at the desk with Jim Prentice, who tried to beckon him over but was flagged down as the DI marched for the stairs. His heart rate ramped up and his collar started to tighten. He yanked off the tie that had caused him so much trouble earlier and spooled the cloth into a ball.

The DI was breathing heavily by the top of the stairs but carried on, past the door to the incident room and onwards to the chief super's office. He ignored the protocol of a knock, opting instead to drop the handle and walk inside.

CS Martin and the chief constable were standing over a desk spread with the morning papers. The predominant image Valentine gleaned from the press was that of Gerald

Fallon being led down the station steps by a uniformed officer who was reaching a splayed hand towards the camera lens.

'Bob, do come in,' said Martin.

'What's going on?' he said.

'We were hoping you could tell us that.'

41

It was perhaps the most placatory Valentine had ever seen the chief super, and he couldn't get used to the new persona. If she was playing down her usual bile to keep him in the job, then her actions were going to prove futile, thought Valentine. With all he'd seen in the last few days, he'd gladly walk away and never return. Transfer or not.

Greaves seemed less concerned with the DI's opinion, heaving himself into Martin's chair and looking over laced fingers at Valentine. 'We seem to have arrived at exactly the point I had hoped to avoid,' said Greaves, waving a hand over the collected press material.

Valentine avoided the remark. 'Why did you release my suspect?'

'Because he wasn't a suspect.'

'I'm the investigating officer. I decide who the suspects are on my investigations.'

'And I'm the chief constable, Bob. Though I'm sure you don't need reminding of that.'

CS Martin stopped fiddling with the coffee machine and headed for the door with the jug in her hand. 'I think I'll get this filled,' she said, holding up the jug on her way out the door.

'What the hell's going on?' said Valentine.

'What on earth do you mean?'

The DI moved closer to the desk. He felt overwhelmed by the piles of bad publicity in front of him. 'Fallon knows something.'

'He wasn't a suspect. We couldn't hold him.'

'He might not have been our murder suspect, but I'm pretty sure he knows who should be top of our list.'

'You can't prove that.'

'And how do you know?'

'Well, can you?'

Valentine smirked as he lowered himself into the vacant seat beyond the desk. 'If you're even asking me that, sir, then you can't be as sure of your position as you think you are.'

'This isn't a game, Bob. It's not about brinkmanship.'

'I know. It's about the deaths of two boys, murdered and sealed in an oil drum for thirty-two years. It's about them, and quite a few more boys like them, and the men who put them there.'

Greaves exhaled slowly and placed his folded hands on the blotter in front of him. His features were still as he spoke again. 'Bob, it's over now. Your suspect killed himself this morning.'

'I was wondering when you were going to mention Garry Keirns,' said Valentine. 'Now that suicide might just turn out to be the most interesting case I've ever worked. You see, sir, I've never known a suicide victim to hoover down his hallway after he's hanged himself.'

'What are you saying to me, Bob? You don't think Keirns killed himself?'

Valentine crossed his legs and brought a firm index finger down on the wooden arm of the chair. 'I think it'll take a few more like Keirns and Trevor Healey being sacrificed before this blows over.'

'Oh really?'

'Yes, sir. The tide has turned.'

CS Martin returned with brisk steps. The jug in her hand was still empty. She thumped it down on the desk and addressed the officers. 'We have a big problem.'

'Tell me about it,' said Valentine.

'No, Bob, things have taken a serious shift since the word got out linking Fallon to Columba House. Protestors are rounding on his home.'

'It's bloody irresponsible reporting,' yelled Greaves. He picked up a newspaper and shook it at Valentine. 'This is insane.'

'I'll get down there right away, before it starts to turn nasty,' said Valentine. The DI left Greaves scrunching the paper into a heap on the desk and headed for the door. When he clasped the handle, there was a knock on the other side.

'Sylvia?' he said.

'Ah, hello, sir.'

'What is it?'

She looked over his shoulder. 'The chief super asked to see me.'

'DS McCormack,' called out Martin. 'If you can just give us five minutes.'

Valentine left the DS standing in the doorway and sprinted to the incident room, calling out for McAlister and Donnelly.

'Yes, sir,' said McAlister. 'What is it this time?'

'If Dino's to be believed it's a march on Racecourse Road by cudgel-carrying protestors,' said Valentine.

'That would be one way of finding justice.'

'Unfortunately, in our business, Ally, we're expected to take a dim view of mob justice.'

They headed for the stairs. On the way out of the station a couple of photographers that had decamped to the rear entrance fired off a few shots in the officers' direction. As the car sped towards the middle of town, one photographer stood staring at the small screen on the back of the camera. Neither man looked pleased with their haul.

Donnelly brought the car to a halt at the foot of the Sandgate, where the traffic had snagged up. As the officers sat at the lights, just shy of the bridge, the radio controller's voice croaked into earshot.

'Looks like a trainload more for the protest just in. Marching towards Miller Road now.'

'They must be advertising this,' said Valentine.

'It's on Facebook, sir,' said McAlister, poring over his iPhone.

'Christ, so is my daughter. I hope she doesn't get any ideas.'

'Quite a few already have, sir. There's anti-capitalists jumping on the bandwagon now.'

'Wait until rent-a-mob finds out Fallon's one of the country types. We'll have the hunt saboteurs next.'

The traffic eased and Donnelly flashed lights to keep a bus driver from pulling out in front of them. The rest of the journey was a stop-start process all the way to Racecourse Road, where a newly erected police cordon indicated a diversion was in progress. The uniformed officers on the cordon waved Donnelly through, towards the growing crowd that had spilled on to the road.

'This is mental,' said Valentine.

'Democracy in action, sir,' replied McAlister.

'Ally, Fallon's not even an elected member any more.'

'I don't think it matters. They're pissed off with the system, and he's a symbol of it.'

Valentine reluctantly conceded the point and ordered the others from the car. Outside Fallon's house a uniformed sergeant approached. 'Are you the backup?' he said.

'Do we look like the bloody riot squad?' said Donnelly. The sight of more police on the scene provoked some rowdy chanting.

'We can't secure the boundary any longer. They're spilling into the garden,' said the sergeant.

'It's only going to get worse when the next trainload get here,' said McAlister.

'There's more on the way?'

'Afraid so, on Miller Road already.'

'This is a bloody disaster waiting to happen.' The sergeant reached for his radio. 'We're going to need all hands to the pump now. And they'll probably have to throw in the canteen staff as well.'

'Scum. Scum. Scum.' The chanting rounded on the officers.

'Right, we're going in,' said Valentine. 'Ally, get round the back door and stay there. Nobody in or out.'

'Yes, sir.'

'And, Phil, we're going in the front. Or should I say, I am. You're on the door once I'm inside.'

'I get all the good jobs.'

The DI patted his shoulder. 'You'll be fine. The cavalry's on the way.'

The team pressed themselves into the crowd and were swallowed up by the swaying mass of bodies. At the main entrance gate two uniformed officers tried to hold back the crowd as the detectives squeezed themselves into the grounds.

Once over the boundary, Valentine had a strange feeling of weightlessness as he lunged into the open space. McAlister and Donnelly appeared directly behind him, brushing themselves down.

'Right, you have your orders.'

As they ran for the building, the DI looked for signs of movement beyond the windows. The curtains were drawn in the lounge downstairs, but the lights appeared to be burning in many of the other rooms. The place looked quiet, unlived in. He wondered if anyone was home.

'Remember, no heroics, Phil,' Valentine said as he reached for the door.

'You too, sir.'

The DI rushed the steps and the front door, closing it behind him. Inside was silent, the main ceiling light and wall lamps all shining to indicate an occupier, but there was no one visible in any direction.

Valentine checked the first door ahead of him. It opened to a large kitchen whose only occupant was a lazy-looking black Lab, curled in a basket by an Aga stove.

'Hello,' said the DI.

There was no reply; the Lab buried its nose in the basket and resumed insouciance.

The DI closed the door and returned to the hallway. The house was quiet, in contrast to the hubbub raging outside; it didn't feel like the same place he had visited earlier. There was a different atmosphere, a stillness that seemed out of place. As he started to walk for the main living room where he had interviewed Fallon, the DI felt his face and hands growing cold, as if he had just walked outside in the depths of winter. He halted. The stillness intensified now, became more like a solid presence that summoned him. As he turned around to face the source Valentine connected at once with the image of a small boy.

Rory Stevenson's pale impression stood at the opposite end of the hallway staring into Valentine's eyes. The boy was motionless – not even an indication of the light flickered in his still gaze.

Valentine's body temperature returned to normal. He felt no fear, only a mute anguish that he knew originated outside of him. As he started to walk towards the boy, the image altered and turned to face the opposite direction. The detective was following him now, down the broad and silent hallway towards another door, where the small boy's image disappeared beyond.

42

The handle was stiff and the door heavy, the old hinges sighing loudly as Valentine pushed forward. The room seemed disproportionately darker than the rest of the house until the detective realised the heavy velveteen curtains were drawn tight across the window. The only other light in the room came from a small, brass desk lamp, its green glass shade throwing off a yellowish glow.

In the hazy light beyond the lamp sat Fallon, slumped in a swivel chair with a heavy glass in one hand. Beside the glass sat a bottle of Glenlivet. It was almost empty. As Valentine approached the desk there was no movement from Fallon at all, as he stared, wide-eyed, into the room's dark recesses. For a moment the DI thought he had found a corpse, until he leaned over the desk and saw Fallon's other hand slowly moving up the stock of the Browning shotgun that was resting in his lap.

The only sound in the musty atmosphere came from a clock ticking somewhere on the bookshelves behind the detective. Beyond the regular tick, tick, tick came an occasional roar from the crowd outside, which was punctuated by the shrill blaring of a car's horn.

When he spoke, Fallon's voice sounded dislocated from the real world. 'She's left.' He looked up, made eye contact with Valentine. 'My wife. She read the papers.'

The DI's pulse was quickening and sweat dampened his forearms. 'You sound surprised.'

'It makes you wonder what it's all for when something like that happens.' Fallon drained the last of his whisky and let the heavy glass fall to the floor; it rolled underneath the desk and out of view.

'And have you reached a conclusion?'

Fallon remained motionless and silent as the noise outside started to rise again. He did not answer the detective.

'Give me the gun,' said Valentine.

'No.'

'You're not going to shoot your way out of this, Fallon.'

'That's not what it's for.'

Valentine leaned on the desk and held out an open hand, making sure all emotion and threat was removed from his voice. 'Come on, give me the gun.'

Fallon pushed himself away from the desk and stepped out of his chair. His finger was on the gun's trigger now. 'I said no.'

The detective eased away and heard the blood pounding in his ears. 'OK, if that's the way you want it.'

'You've got this all wrong you know, Valentine. All wrong.'

'That's funny, Garry Keirns told me that as well. Before he was killed.'

'Bloody Keirns.' Fallon spat the name. 'He was always letting his mouth run.'

'Is that why he was killed?'

Fallon dipped his head and formed a lopsided grin. 'You'll be accusing me of that next, I suppose.'

'Well, did you?'

'That idiot got himself killed. I can't even say he was a useful idiot in the end.' He lowered the gun and placed it on the desk between himself and Valentine, but kept his hand on the barrel. 'Look, Keirns knew a little, and you know what they say – a little knowledge is a dangerous thing. But he didn't know the whole story – nothing bloody like it!'

'What's the whole story then? Why don't you tell me?'

Fallon rubbed the back of his neck as if easing out cramp. As he moved, the motion rocked the gun on the desk. 'Not what you think. That picture you showed me, that's nothing to do with it. Nothing to do with all of this mess.'

As the former MP spoke, Valentine became aware that Fallon was dressed very formally in a fitted dress suit and tie. The collars of his white shirt were stiff and starched, fastened low on his neck by a large Windsor knot. There was a pin in the tie – a red garnet stone, very like the one in the signet ring he was now wearing on the little finger of his right hand.

'When I first came here with DS McAlister, you were wearing gloves,' said Valentine. 'You thought you'd get away with keeping them on when we went inside, but then you saw me looking at them and turned away to take them off.'

Fallon held up the ring. 'You couldn't have seen it. I took it off inside my driving gloves, and I was careful to leave it in there.'

251

'I thought that's what you'd done.'

Fallon lowered his hand and put it in his pocket. 'Keirns told me about the picture, you know, but it was nothing to do with this absurd affair. I swear to you that was something different. I've never killed a child.'

'Someone did. Someone killed two young boys who made the mistake of being alive and in the wrong place at the wrong time.'

'And you think that was me?'

'If not you then who?'

Fallon turned to face the other wall, pointing to a small oil painting of a yacht in a gilt frame. It was a colourful summer scene, with cloudless blue skies above and crystal-clear waters below, lapping at the bow of the boat. It seemed an image as far removed from the current situation as possible. 'In there – the safe. Open it.'

'What will I find?'

'The answer you're looking for.'

Valentine was uneasy turning his back on the man but walked to the other side of the room and took down the delicate painting with some care. Behind the frame was an indent in the wall where there sat a small grey security box with a black handle.

Fallon spoke. 'The key's in it. Turn the handle.'

As Valentine opened the small, square door a bolt mechanism clicked into place. He looked inside and saw a long, cylindrical cardboard roll.

'Take it out and bring it over here.' Fallon stayed at the desk by the gun, watching every one of the detective's slow and careful movements.

Valentine removed the roll and returned to the desk,

placing the item under the light from the lamp. He watched as Fallon opened up the scroll and threw down a bundle of faded colour photographs that were attached with a paperclip.

'There you go,' he said, stepping away from the desk as if to disassociate himself. 'You won't see me in any of them.'

In the first picture the detective identified Rory Stevenson straightaway. Rory was with an unknown, bare-chested man. The same man featured in the second picture that was removed, and also the third. There were more pictures, but Valentine didn't need to look at them to know what they contained. He threw down the pile of photographs in disgust and turned to face Fallon.

'Speak,' said the detective.

'Recognise the man?'

'Who is it?'

'It's Andrew Lucas. I don't think I need to tell you who the boy is. We all know he's the reason we're here.'

Valentine struggled with the rage building in him. 'What the hell is this, Fallon?'

Fallon grabbed the pictures and started to flick through them. His voice came loudly, his words rapidly firing; he'd held the secret inside him for too long and wanted to be rid of it now. 'Andy Lucas and the murdered boy at Ardinsh Farm . . . Andy Lucas with two murdered boys, in the same place . . . ' He flung down the photographs as he went. They slapped on to the desk and skidded into a grim montage of flesh and depravity.

Valentine reached out and grabbed Fallon's hands. 'Enough. Do you hear me, you bastard? I said enough!'

Fallon stepped away. 'It wasn't me. I told you, and that's your proof.'

'How did it happen? Why?' He reached for Fallon's shoulders now and spun him around.

'How? Jesus, isn't it blindingly obvious, man?'

'I think I can make out the seedy perverts' sex party, maybe even see how the Columba House boy ends up there, but how does Rory Stevenson fit in and why?'

Fallon bunched a handful of his iron-grey hair. The long strands lay limply on his moist brow as he retreated to his chair. 'The boys were regulars at a certain sort of soiree Garry Keirns ran back then.'

'At Ardinsh Farm?'

'Well yes. But not exclusively. This time, though, yes.'

'This time? What do you mean by that?'

'They were numerous, these nights in, and Andy Lucas was a regular. That's why I was brought . . . Lucas was becoming very powerful in his little fiefdom then. He needed to be secured.'

'Blackmailed you mean?'

'Christ, don't be naive. Do you think people like Lucas can be moved around like useful little chess pieces? This is how the world turns.'

'And you were just helping out, were you? Just doing your bit. Keeping everything hush-hush to make sure it was business as usual for all your slimy friends.'

'Do you think I had a choice? You've seen the evidence.' He scattered the photographs over the desk.

Valentine grabbed Fallon's hand and shoved it away from the photographs. 'Who killed the boys? Tell me everything.'

Fallon patted his ribcage and slid his fingers into the tight pocket of the waistcoat beneath his dress jacket. 'I believe it was Lucas. I believe it was unintentional.' He seemed resigned now, not relieved, but familiar enough with the facts of the case to know that he had no way of withholding what he knew any longer. If he didn't reveal these secrets, he might incriminate himself, and that was something Fallon, a born survivor, would never do.

'One was strangled and one bludgeoned to death. How in God's name can that be unintentional?' said Valentine.

'There was some kind of mix-up. The Stevenson boy was brought along by mistake and reacted, well, appropriately.'

'He was coshed for objecting to what he saw, you mean?'

'My understanding is there was some kind of squabble, yes. The other one came to his aid and was subdued by Lucas. Unfortunately he didn't know his own strength and the boy couldn't be revived.'

Valentine touched his mouth. He felt as if he wanted to push in his words. His sudden understanding projected images he didn't want to see, even if it meant he had the answers now. His words escaped angrily. 'And Lucas couldn't keep Rory around to identify him after that.'

'Obviously not. I mean it stands to reason that was the thinking behind it.'

'So the boys get dumped in a barrel and then a shallow grave. How very clinical and convenient for you and your cronies.'

'It wasn't supposed to happen that way. It was supposed to be all about applying a bit of pressure to Lucas. Nobody wanted to see those boys killed.'

'You make it sound so bloody matter of fact. Two boys

died here, and Christ alone knows how many more were raped and abused as part of your little sting operation, Fallon.'

'It wasn't as simple as that. It wasn't my doing,' he pleaded.

'You let it go on, didn't you?'

'What could I do about it?'

'What could you . . .' Valentine felt his pulse returning to normal as he looked at the distraught image of Fallon slumping into himself. He was wrecked, half a lifetime of secrets and lies coming back to destroy him. Fallon was spent, a hollow of a man, without any hint of the arrogance he'd used to hide the horrific truth of the life he had lived.

'Get up.'

'Please, Detective.' He indicated the gun with a nod. 'Just leave me alone. Just for a moment longer.'

'Another convenient solution in mind?'

'We both know how this looks.'

'Is that all that matters to you?'

He lowered his head and sighed. 'Nothing matters now.'

Valentine steadied himself. 'Is it loaded?'

Fallon made a weak nod. 'Yes.'

'I think that's actually something I'd like to see,' said Valentine. 'Though perhaps not as much as I'd like to see you begging for your eternal soul.'

'I'll beg you for your mercy, if that's what you want me to do.'

The detective stepped forward and raised the gun from its resting place on the desk. He kept Fallon in his gaze as he lowered the gun out of his line of sight and moved away.

'No one showed those boys any mercy. No one paid their fate a second thought. There'll be no easy way out for you this time, Fallon. I hope you burn in hell, but before that I hope you have a long time to savour your fate on this earth.'

43
Epilogue

The mood around the breakfast table was more sombre than usual. At first Valentine thought it was the television news report detailing the arrest of Gerald Fallon and the reopening of the Columba House investigation that was the cause. He had risen from his point at the head of the table and turned off the television, only to discover his father had a radio playing in the extension that was warning of the continued closure of Racecourse Road.

'The vandals have got in now,' said Valentine's father, emerging from the extension and putting a cup in the sink.

'I'd say that's the least of his worries,' said Valentine.

'Och, I know. It's the fact that they've spray-painted all his sordid activities over the sandstone – and on the wall outside too. Kiddies go to school down that way. It's not right they should see that kind of thing.'

'The road's closed, Dad.'

'Will your boys clean it up?'

'No. That's the council's area I'm afraid.'

His father shrugged and took his place at the table. 'I thought I might put some flowers on Sandy's grave today.'

'That's a nice thought,' said Clare, reaching out for the coffee pot and placing it in front of her.

'I don't assume I'll be alone. There'll be a pile of flowers likely.'

Valentine drained his cup and pushed out his chair. He'd spent long enough thinking about the case of late and how it had reached into the community, tearing out more emotions as it went. 'I'm off.'

'Call me as soon as you hear anything,' said Clare.

'It's too soon, love. Give it time.'

His wife glanced at the ceiling like she was inwardly counting to ten. 'Well, call anyway.'

Valentine placed a kiss on Clare's head and left for the station. As he threw his coat on the back seat of the Vectra he caught a glimpse of the dark stain covering the upholstery. He hadn't looked at the place where he had bled after his stabbing for a long time; the sight of the stain had once terrified his daughters – who begged him to get rid of the car – but they no longer talked about it. Was it possible everyone was moving on?

The road into Ayr was busy, filled with commuter traffic and the late influx of tourists brought by the better weather. The sun was warm today, pressing itself on to the world and renewing optimism of better days to come.

By King Street Valentine's thought patterns had synchronised with the climate and he felt, if not glad to be back, content to try and get through another shift. He couldn't say he wanted to be there, and after everything he'd witnessed recently, he couldn't say he wanted to repeat any of it, but he knew his team had succeeded where so many others had failed. Was that something like pride he felt?

'Morning, Bob,' said Jim Prentice. He was in relaxed pose, leaning over the countertop and staring at the pages of a tabloid newspaper. 'I see they're reopening the house-of-horrors case then.'

'It has to be done, no question about it,' said Valentine.

'Maybe we'll get it right this time.' A note of shame sounded in the desk sergeant's voice.

'Well, the odds are tipped a little more in our favour now.' As the DI spoke he realised that this was a conversation he didn't want to have. By the look on Prentice's face, he felt the same.

'Those bloody poor boys,' he said.

'Makes you question everything, doesn't it?' Valentine headed for the stairs. He managed to get at least halfway there when the desk sergeant called out to him again.

'Oh, Bob, did you hear?' His tone had altered, seemed higher.

'Hear what?'

'About Greavsie. They've put him on gardening leave.'

'The chief constable?'

'Well, I'm not talking about the old Spurs player! Yes, Bill Greaves is off, and the word on the street is he's not coming back.'

Valentine felt his mood lifting even higher. 'You have a good day there, Jim.'

'Oh I will.'

At the top of the stairs the DI found he was still grinning to himself, though he didn't know rightly why he should be. He was heading into the incident room to check in with the murder squad when he was waylaid by the chief super, beckoning him from her office door with a confident bark.

'Bob, in here . . .'

He turned round and walked in the other direction, keeping his pace slow and restrained in case it might be interpreted as enthusiasm. 'Good morning, boss,' he said.

'Come in and shut the door behind you.'

Valentine moved towards the middle of the room where CS Martin's desk sat in front of the large square window with the view of the King Street roundabout and the council flats opposite. He descended into the opposing chair, crossing his legs beneath the line of the desk.

'You won't have heard about the chief constable yet,' said Martin.

'Gardening leave.'

'You have? Who in the . . .' She interrupted herself, 'Bloody Jim "the gas" Prentice, no doubt.'

'I couldn't possibly comment.'

'Well yes, gardening leave, but it isn't really.'

'Oh no?'

'No. Let's just say that's the official version of events. I think it's more accurate to say we're having the gold clock engraved with "thanks for the memories" as we speak.'

'I see. I'm sure he'll be well looked after . . . The clock aside, of course,' said Valentine. He gripped the armrests and started to rise. 'Was that everything?'

'No. Stay where you are.' Martin picked up a yellow pencil and started to tap the sharpened point into the desk blotter. 'You'll know by now the Met's investigation into historical child abuse is taking an interest in the Columba House case.'

'We've already exchanged information with them. They seem particularly interested in the Westminster links we've unearthed,' said Valentine.

'And we've a better chance of securing Fallon's conviction with their cooperation, so bear that in mind too.'

'Yes, chief.' He started to edge out of his seat again.

'Just a minute, I'm not finished with you yet.' Martin reached into a drawer in her desk and withdrew a large manila envelope and slapped it down in front of Valentine. 'I want you to have a look at this.'

He reached out and retrieved the envelope. 'What's in here?'

'It's my alternative offer, something you might want to consider instead of a transfer back to Tulliallan and the stink of sweaty jockstraps and Deep Heat.'

The DI removed the small bunch of stapled pages inside. He read the opening rubric slowly, then read it again to make sure he'd got it right. 'You want me to consider a new DCI role?'

'That's right, Bob. More money, less stress, and absolutely no chance of the kind of boredom you know you'll face at the training college.'

Valentine thumbed through the pages carefully. It was a typical move by the chief super, but he hadn't seen it coming. He felt slightly aggrieved with himself for not preparing a ready rebuttal, something suitably cryptic that would see Martin creasing her brows and wondering why she had made the offer in the first place.

'I can't accept this,' he said.

'And why not?'

'For a start, you said yourself that there's no one else ready to take over the DI's role.'

'And as you reminded me, DS McCormack's more than capable. I've assessed her already, before you ask, and she's up for it.'

The DI found himself unable to disagree. 'Sylvia's a good copper.'

'Then you'll accept?'

'No. I'm sorry.' His response had a ring of finality. 'You don't understand what I was asking you for.'

'I do, Bob, trust me. You're feeling burnt out, fatigued . . .'

'It's not that. It's my wife and my home life – or lack thereof.'

'Bob, I know all that. And I also know you can't afford to retire. I've run the numbers and there's no way you can comfortably go down the pay scale and retire any time soon. In your position you need to maximise all the working life that you have left in you.'

It was a low move. What Martin was really reminding him was that he'd suffered a serious injury to his heart – his lifespan after normal retirement age might not be what he thought it was. Even though he knew this fact, had replayed it in his own mind many times, it was something he had tried hard to ignore.

'I just can't agree to this, not now,' said Valentine. 'Clare has my word, and I can't go back on that.'

CS Martin pushed herself away from the edge of the desk, rolling on her chair's castors towards the window. She stood up and stared into the street with her back towards the DI. 'That's fine, I understand. Why don't you take some time off, go on a holiday and talk it over with Clare. But choose your moment wisely.'

The bright sun was hitting the windowpane, painting a hazy glow around the silhouette of the chief super. A holiday never seemed more appealing.

'You know what?' said Valentine. 'I think I might just do that.'